THE MONSTER PIANO

by C. Pitcher

ILLUSTRATED BY BRIDGET MACKEITH

Librarian Reviewer
Allyson A.W. Lyga
Library Media/Graphic Novel Consultant
Fulbright Memorial Fund Scholar, author

Reading Consultant
Elizabeth Stedem
Educator/Consultant, Colorado Springs, CO
MA in Elementary Education, University of Denver, CO

STONE ARCH BOOKS
Minneapolis   San Diego

First published in the United States in 2007
by Stone Arch Books,
151 Good Counsel Drive, P.O. Box 669,
Mankato, Minnesota 56002.
www.stonearchbooks.com

Originally published in Great Britain in 2002
by A & C Black Publishers Ltd,
38 Soho Square, London, W1D 3HB.

Library of Congress Cataloging-in-Publication Data
Pitcher, Caroline.
[Please Don't Eat My Sister!]
The Monster Piano / by C. Pitcher; illustrated by Bridget MacKeith.
p. cm. — (Graphic Trax)
Originally published with the title: Please Don't Eat My Sister! 2002.
ISBN-13: 978-1-59889-087-7 (hardcover)
ISBN-10: 1-59889-087-5 (hardcover)
ISBN-13: 978-1-59889-233-8 (paperback)
ISBN-10: 1-59889-233-9 (paperback)
1. Graphic novels. I. MacKeith, Bridget. II. Title. III. Series.
PN6737.P58P64 2007
741.5'941—dc22 2006006070

Summary: Can a piano be a monster? This one can! Lenny has to convince the rest of his family that his little sister is in real danger from the new grand piano in the living room.

Art Director: Heather Kindseth
Colorists: Michelle Biedscheid and Kathy Clobes
Graphic Designer: Kay Fraser
Production Artist: Keegan Gilbert

1 2 3 4 5 6 11 10 09 08 07 06

Printed in the United States of America.

TABLE OF CONTENTS

Cast of Characters

LENNY

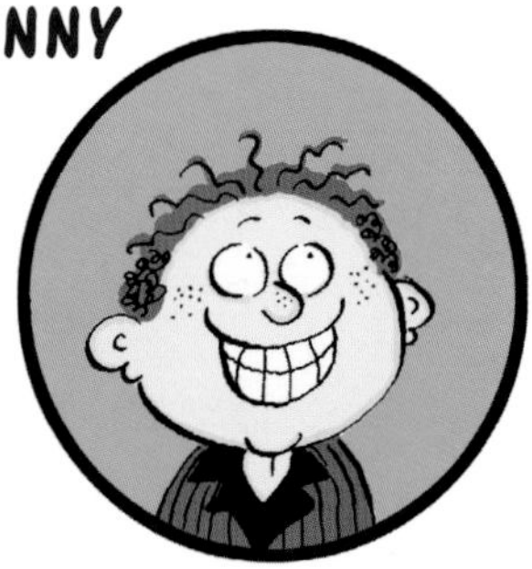

LOUISE

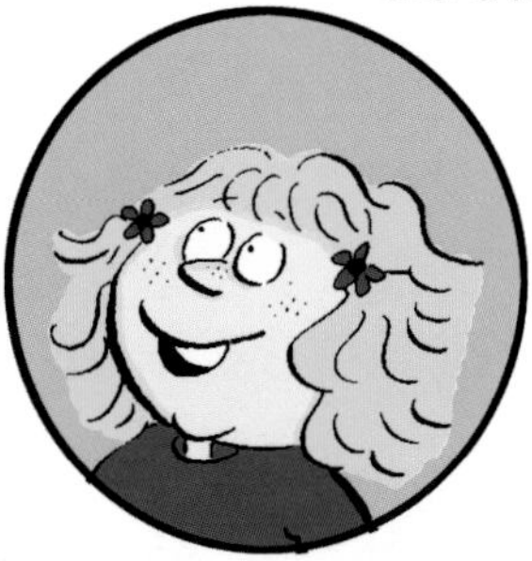

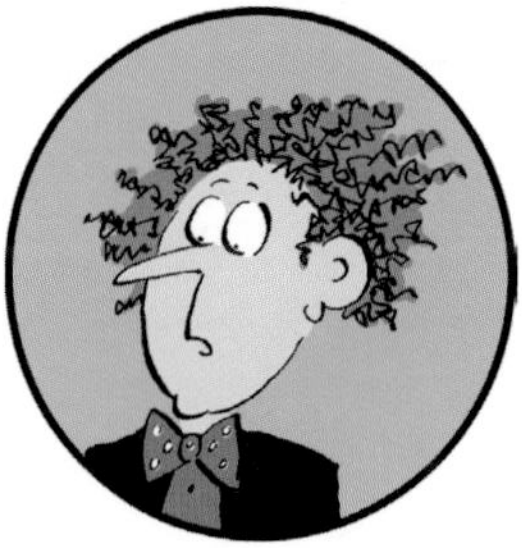

MR. BLATT

THE GRAND PIANO

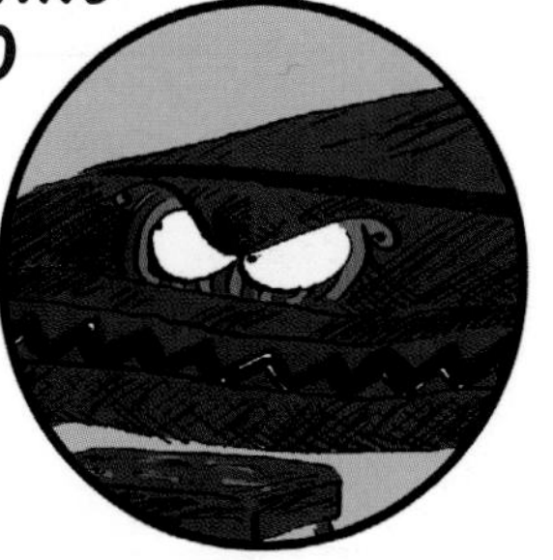

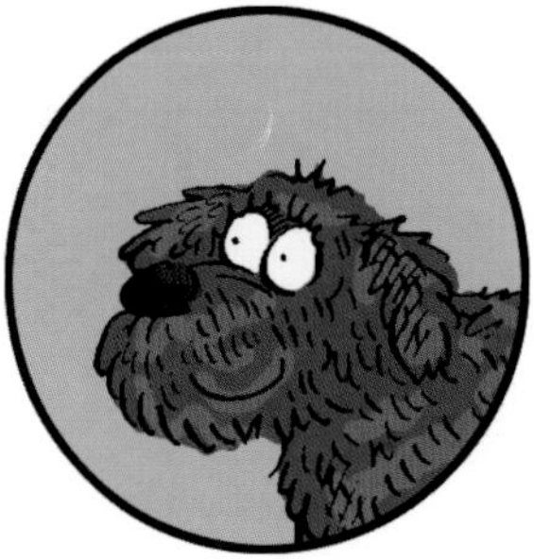

BONZO

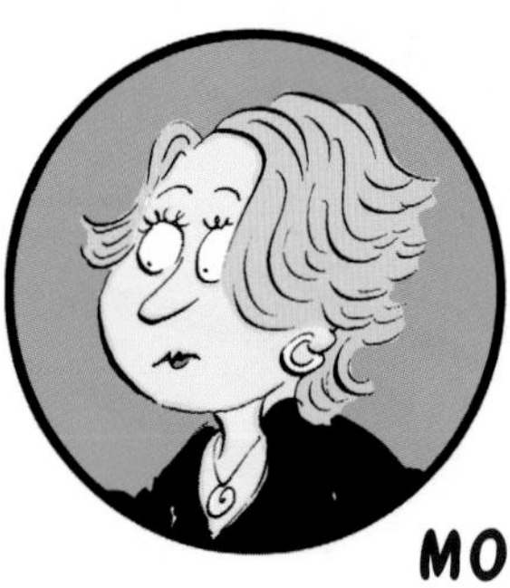

MOM

Chapter One

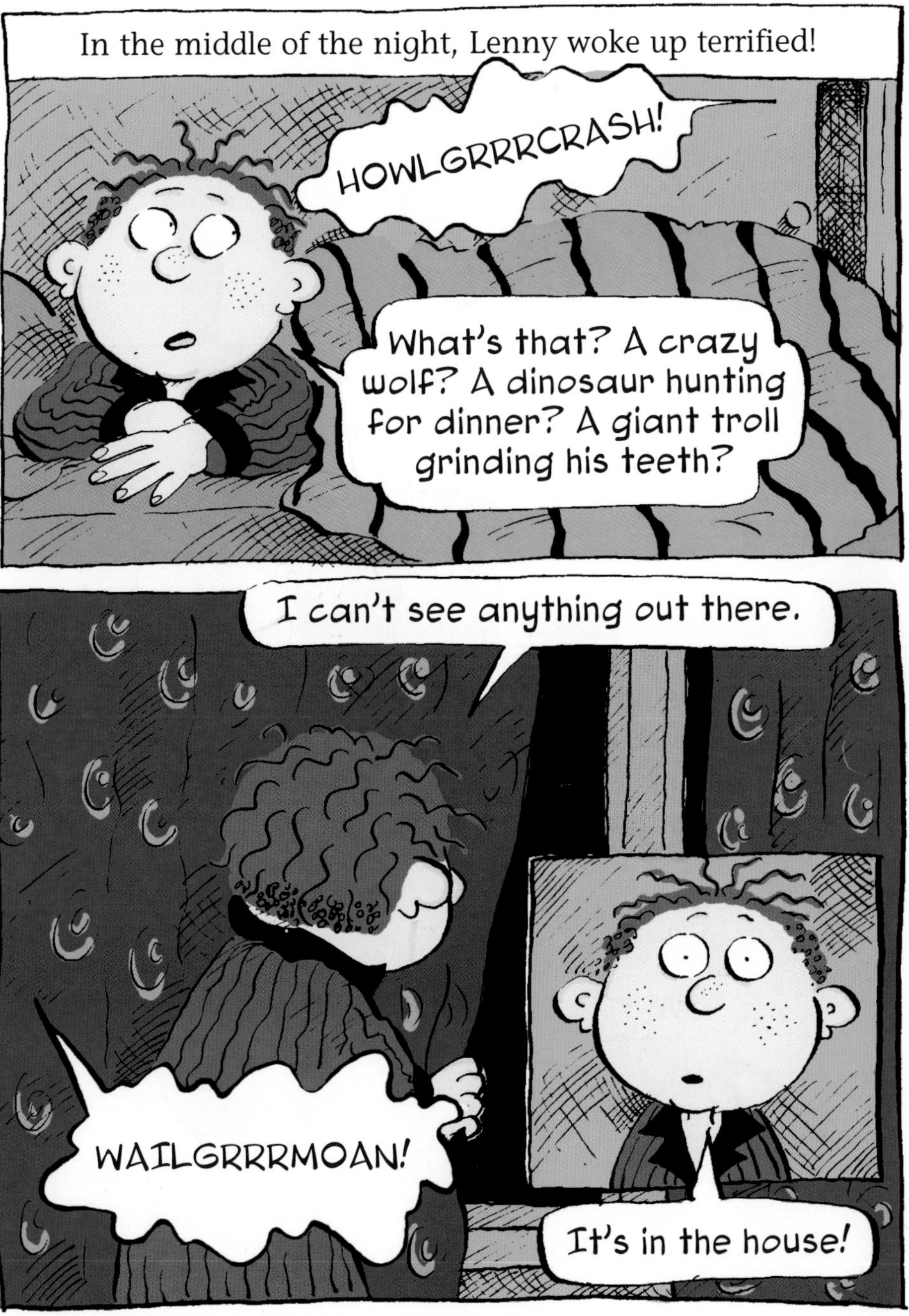
In the middle of the night, Lenny woke up terrified!
HOWLGRRRCRASH!
What's that? A crazy wolf? A dinosaur hunting for dinner? A giant troll grinding his teeth?
I can't see anything out there.
WAILGRRRMOAN!
It's in the house!

Lenny crept to the top of the stairs. He could see something crouching at the bottom. It was shivering. It looked up at Lenny with big, white eyes.

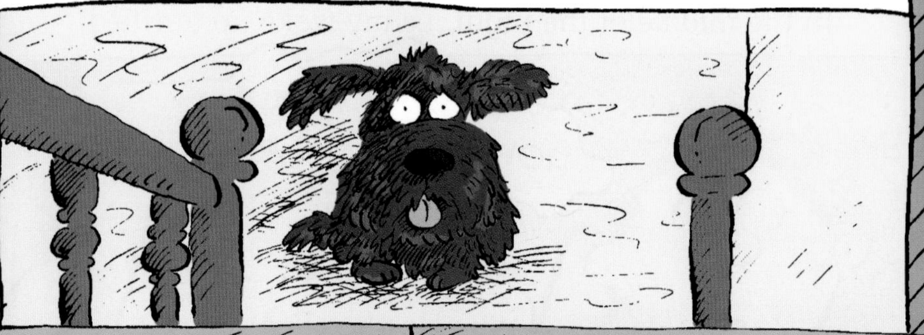

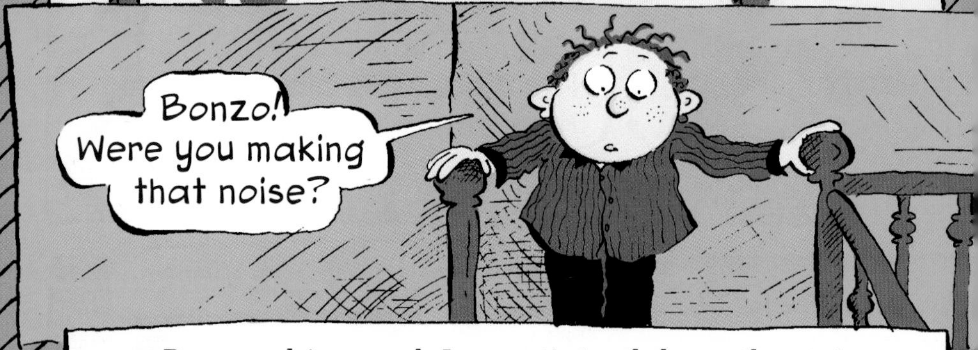
Bonzo! Were you making that noise?

Bonzo whimpered. Lenny tiptoed down the stairs.

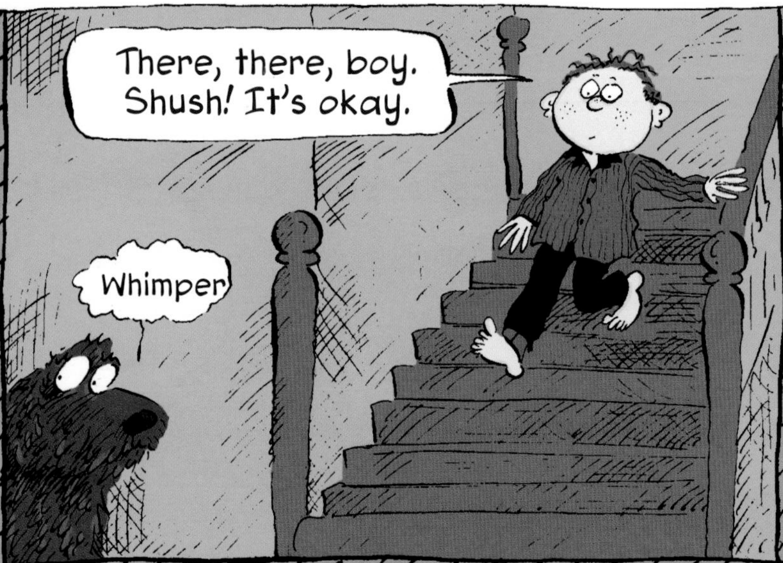
There, there, boy. Shush! It's okay.
Whimper

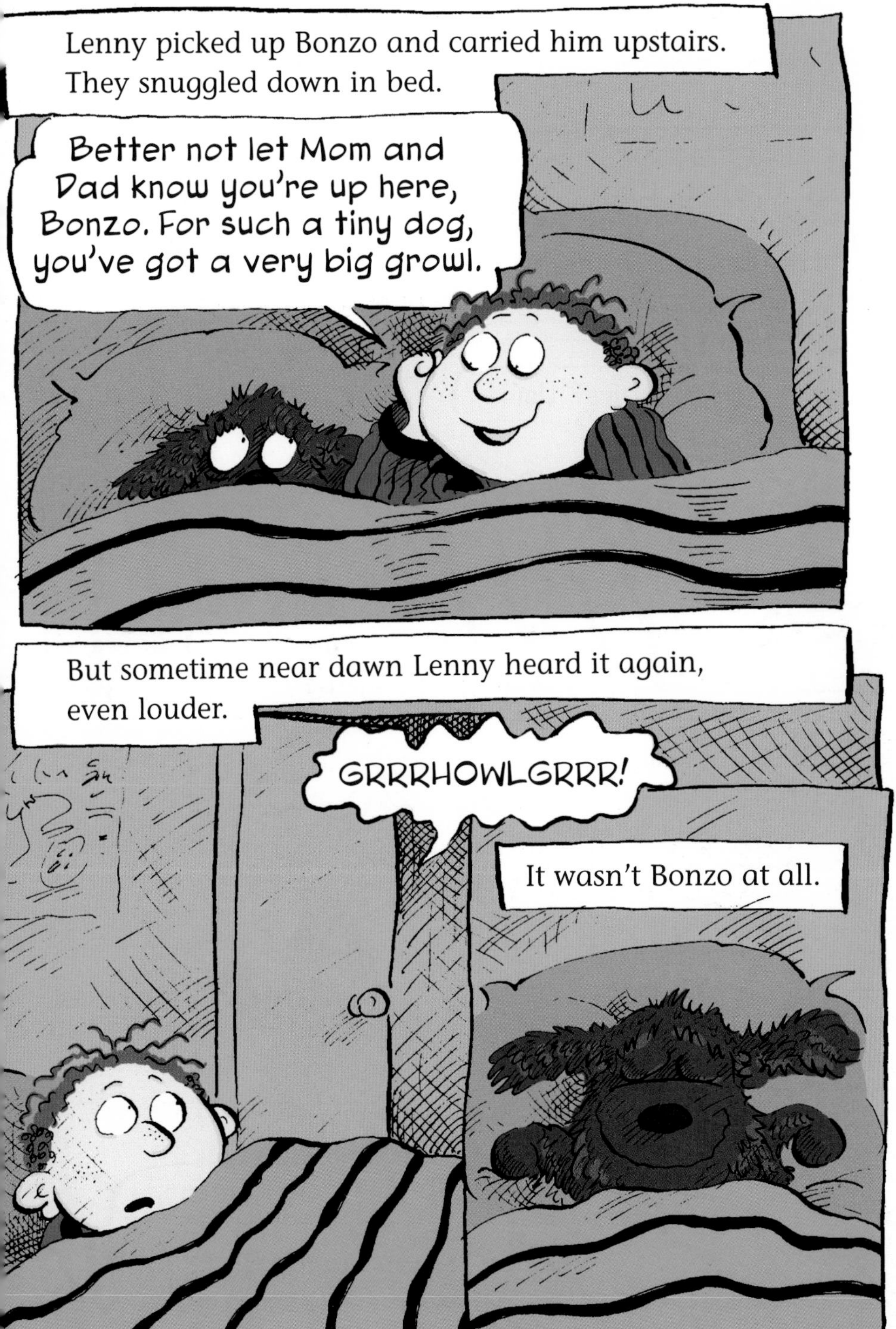
Lenny picked up Bonzo and carried him upstairs. They snuggled down in bed.
Better not let Mom and Dad know you're up here, Bonzo. For such a tiny dog, you've got a very big growl.
But sometime near dawn Lenny heard it again, even louder.
GRRRHOWLGRRR!
It wasn't Bonzo at all.

Chapter Two

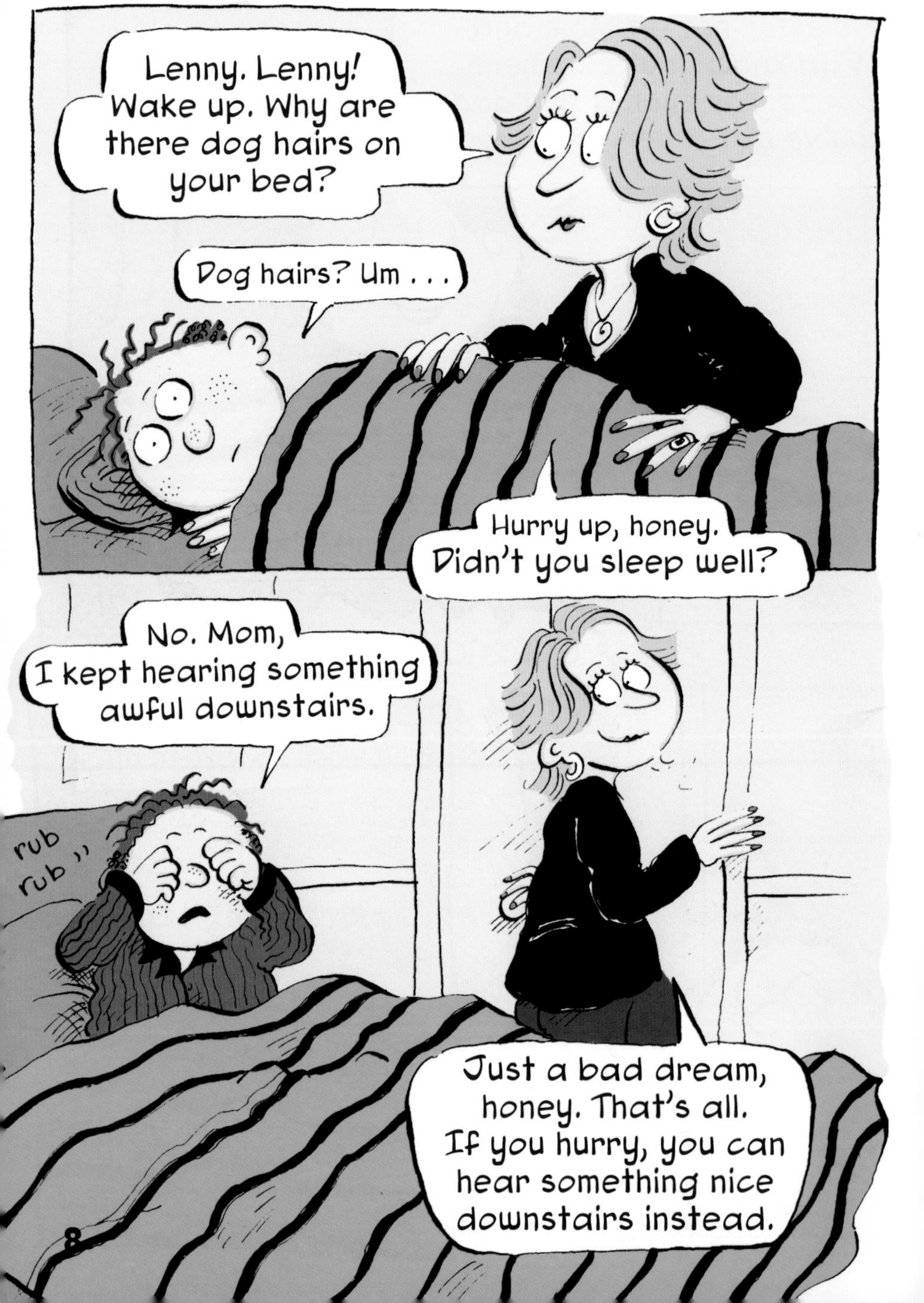

Lenny. Lenny! Wake up. Why are there dog hairs on your bed?
Dog hairs? Um . . .
Hurry up, honey. Didn't you sleep well?
No. Mom, I kept hearing something awful downstairs.
rub rub
Just a bad dream, honey. That's all. If you hurry, you can hear something nice downstairs instead.

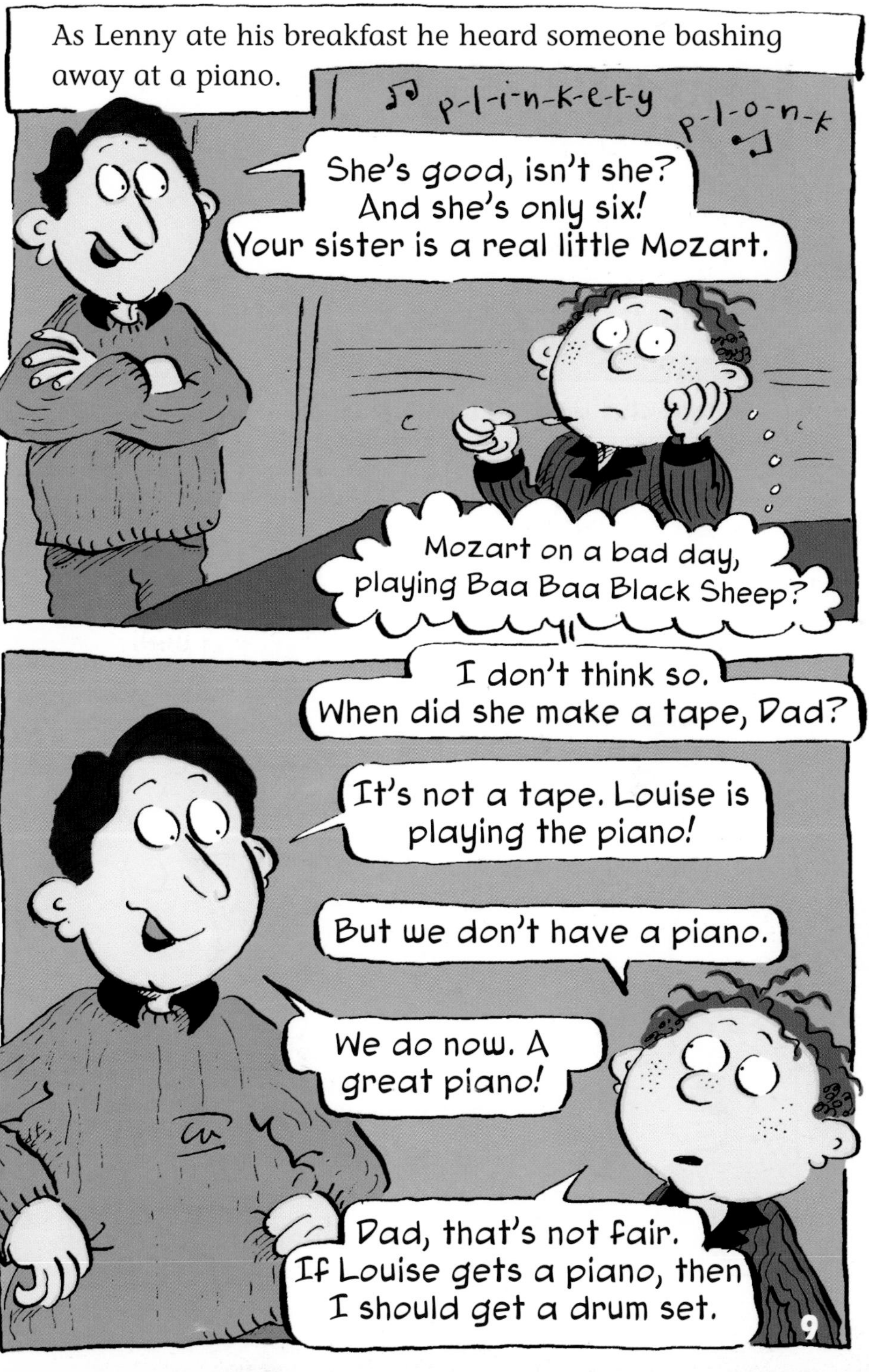
As Lenny ate his breakfast he heard someone bashing away at a piano.
p-l-i-n-k-e-t-y p-l-o-n-k
She's good, isn't she? And she's only six! Your sister is a real little Mozart.
Mozart on a bad day, playing Baa Baa Black Sheep?
I don't think so. When did she make a tape, Dad?
It's not a tape. Louise is playing the piano!
But we don't have a piano.
We do now. A great piano!
Dad, that's not fair. If Louise gets a piano, then I should get a drum set.

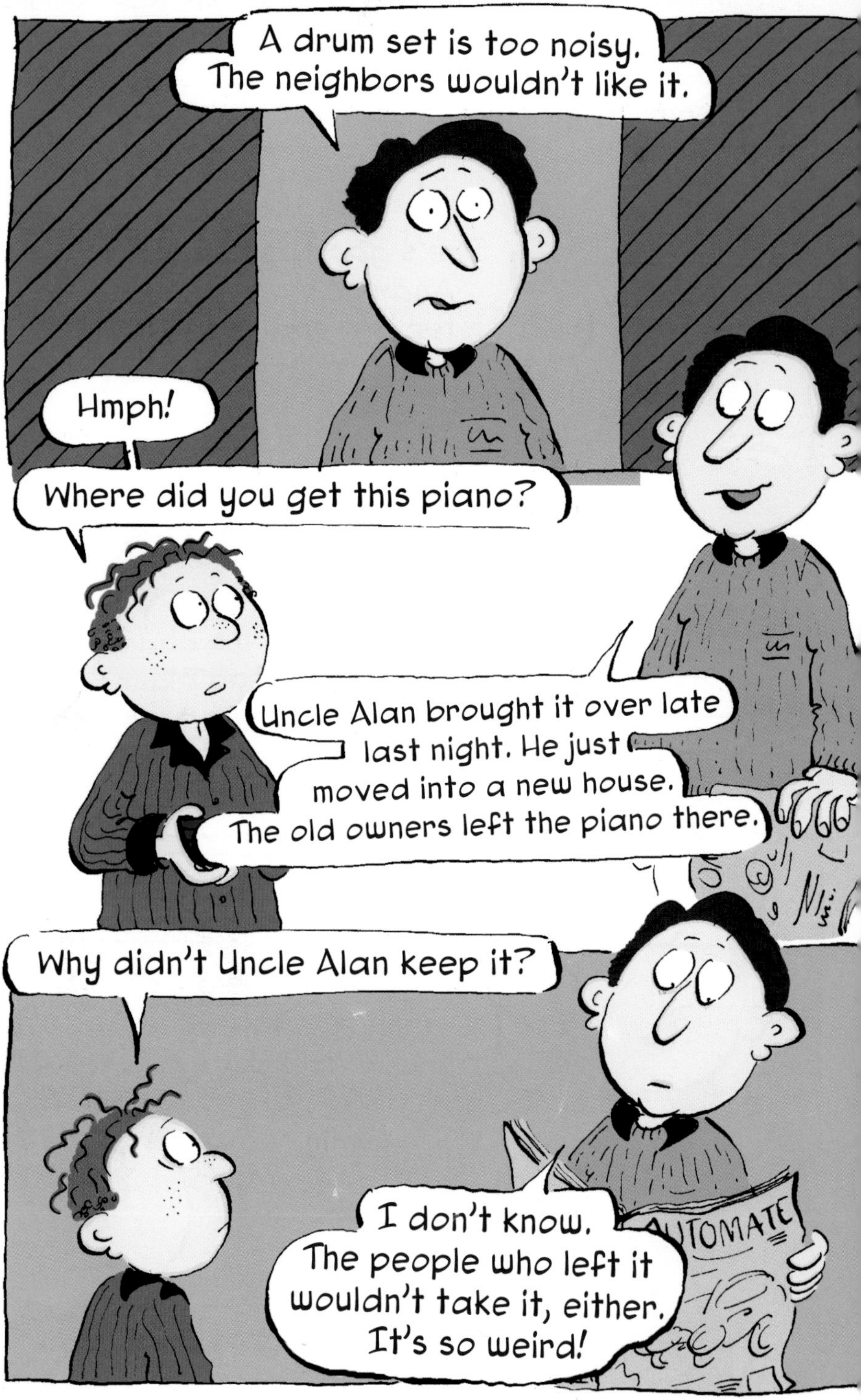
A drum set is too noisy. The neighbors wouldn't like it.
Hmph!
Where did you get this piano?
Uncle Alan brought it over late last night. He just moved into a new house. The old owners left the piano there.
Why didn't Uncle Alan keep it?
I don't know. The people who left it wouldn't take it, either. It's so weird!
AUTOMATE

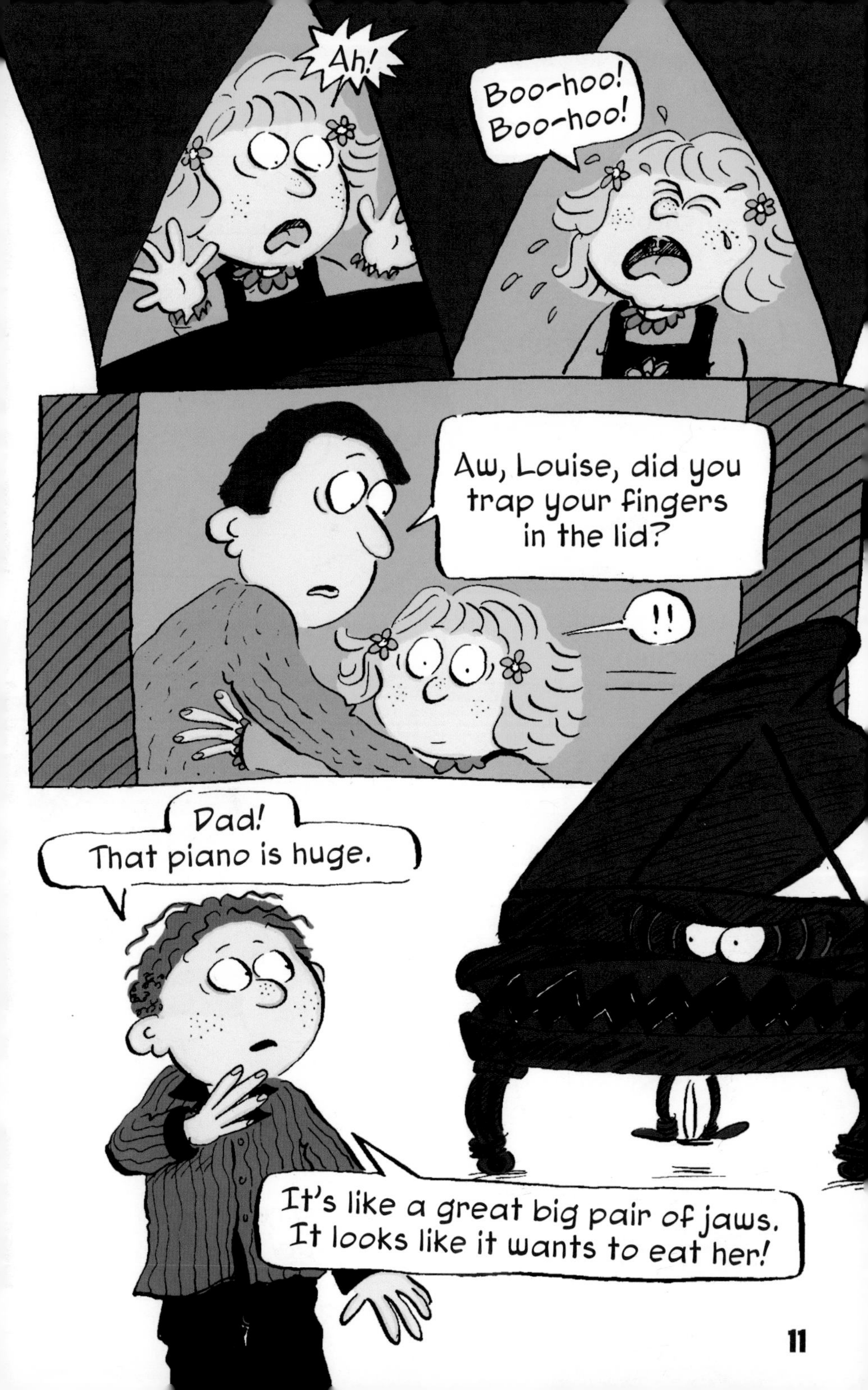
Ah!
Boo-hoo! Boo-hoo!
Aw, Louise, did you trap your fingers in the lid?
!!
Dad! That piano is huge.
It's like a great big pair of jaws. It looks like it wants to eat her!

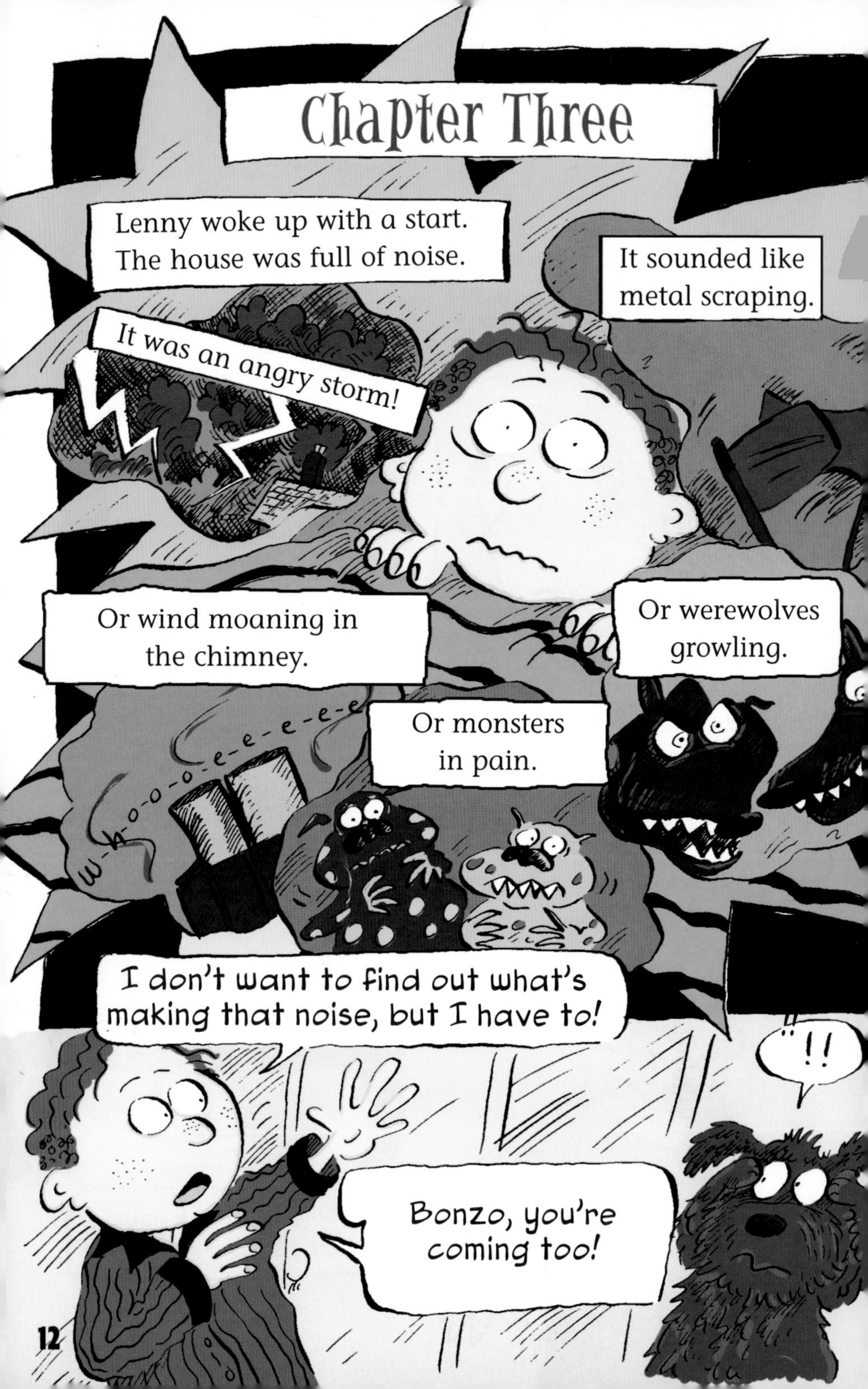
Chapter Three
Lenny woke up with a start. The house was full of noise.
It sounded like metal scraping.
It was an angry storm!
Or wind moaning in the chimney.
Or werewolves growling.
w-h-o-o-o-o-e-e-e-e-e
Or monsters in pain.
I don't want to find out what's making that noise, but I have to!
!!
Bonzo, you're coming too!

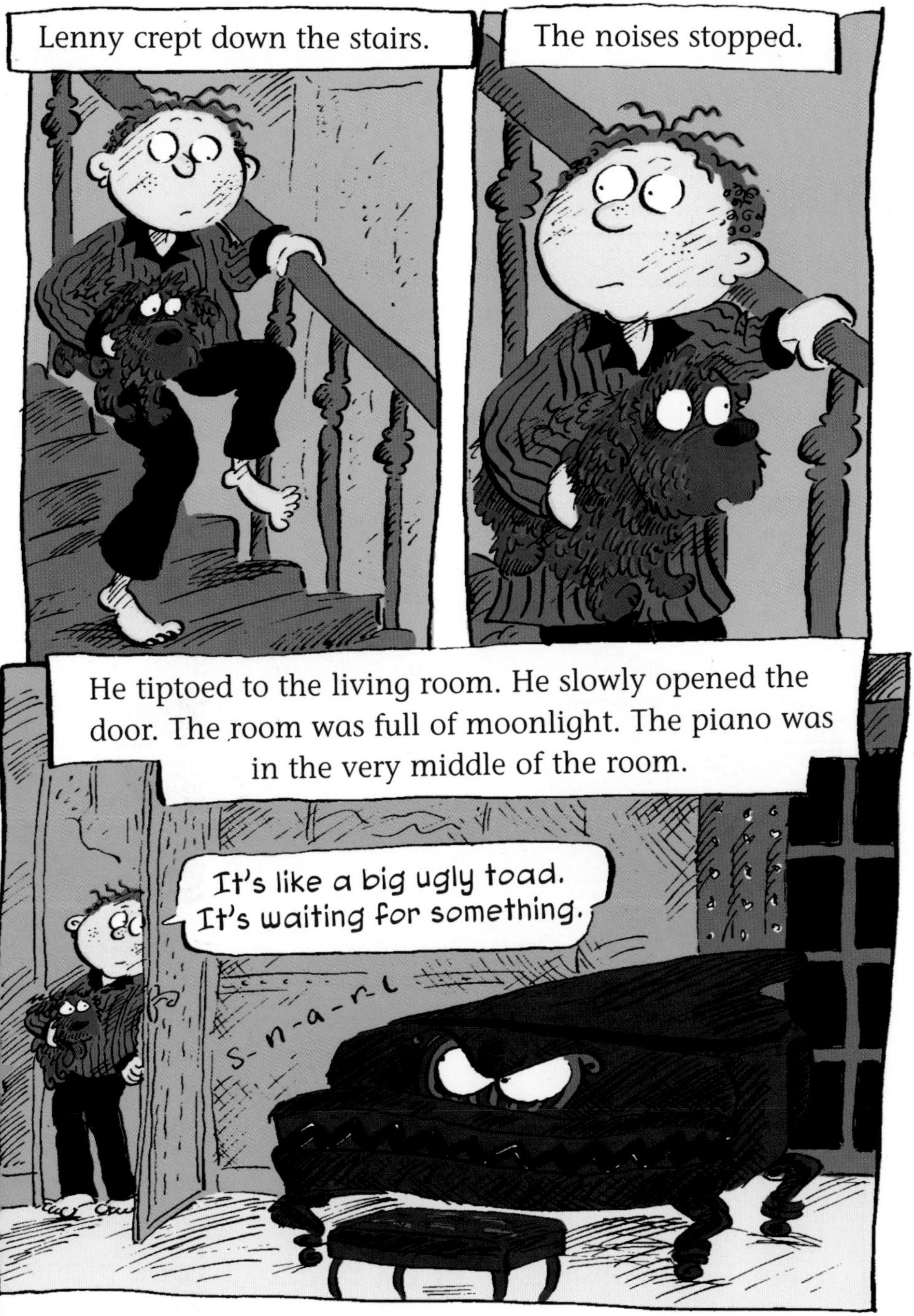
Lenny crept down the stairs.
The noises stopped.
He tiptoed to the living room. He slowly opened the door. The room was full of moonlight. The piano was in the very middle of the room.
It's like a big ugly toad. It's waiting for something.
s-n-a-r-l

Lenny wondered what the piano was waiting for.

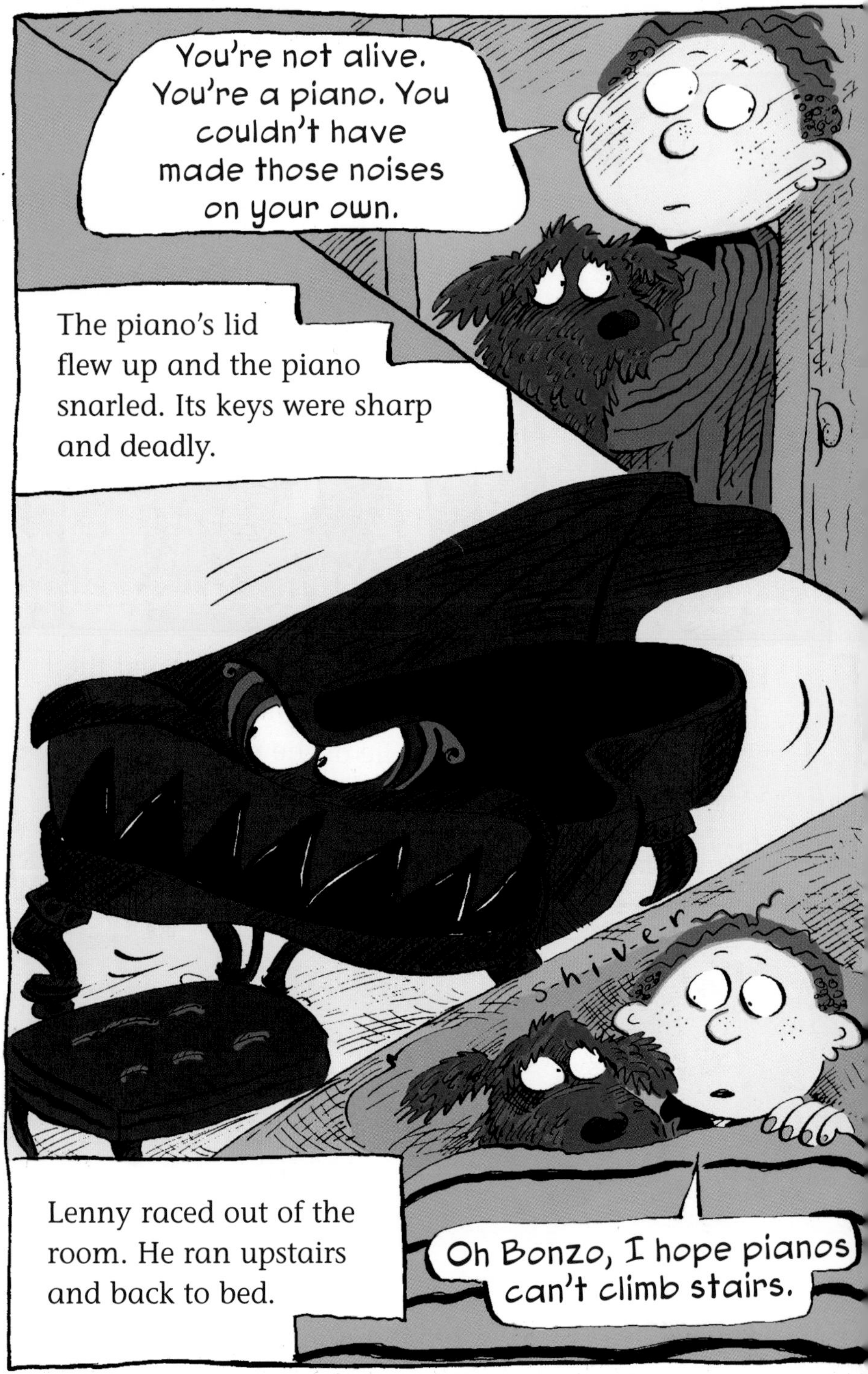
You're not alive. You're a piano. You couldn't have made those noises on your own.
The piano's lid flew up and the piano snarled. Its keys were sharp and deadly.
s-h-i-v-e-r
Lenny raced out of the room. He ran upstairs and back to bed.
Oh Bonzo, I hope pianos can't climb stairs.

Chapter Four

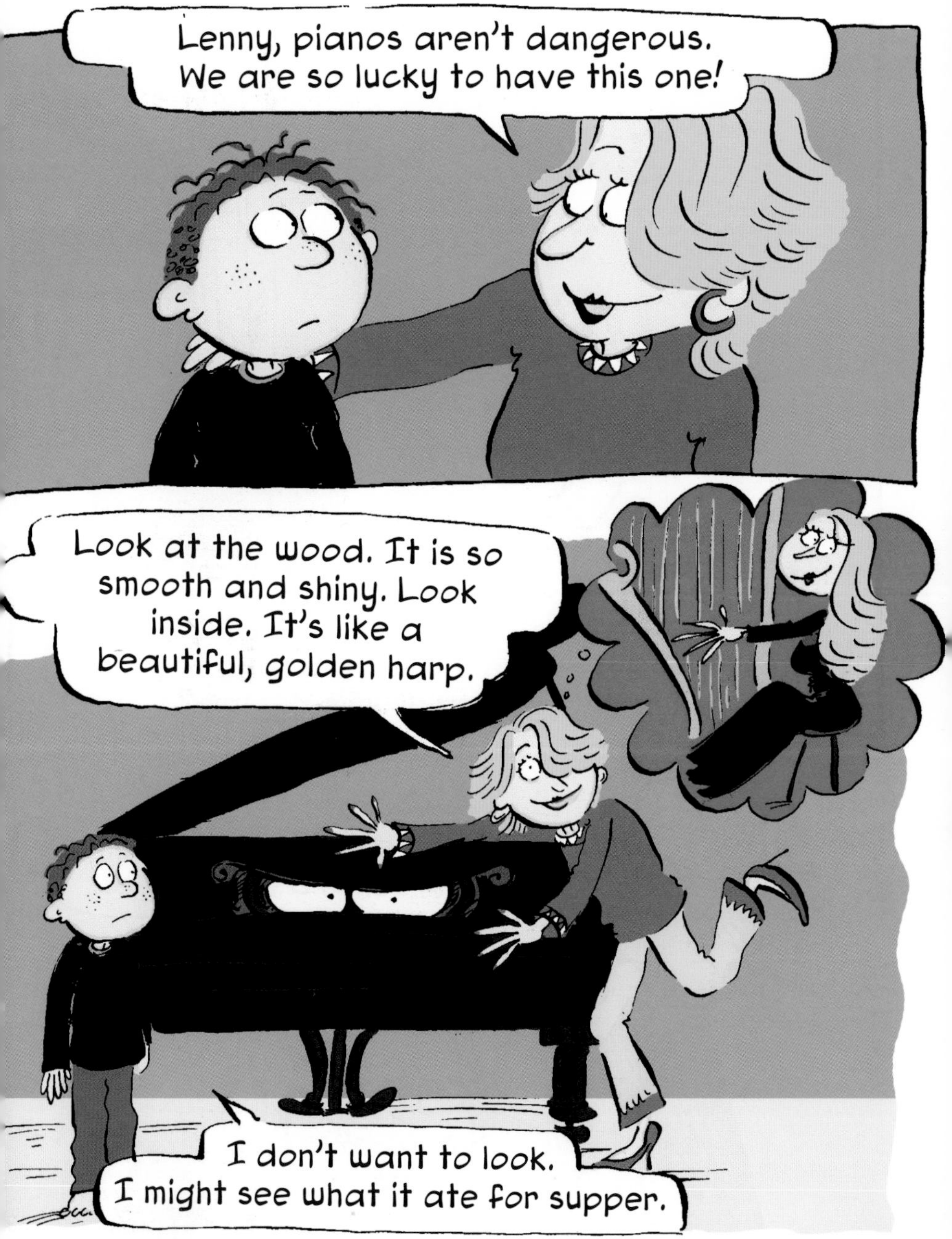
Lenny, pianos aren't dangerous. We are so lucky to have this one!
Look at the wood. It is so smooth and shiny. Look inside. It's like a beautiful, golden harp.
I don't want to look. I might see what it ate for supper.

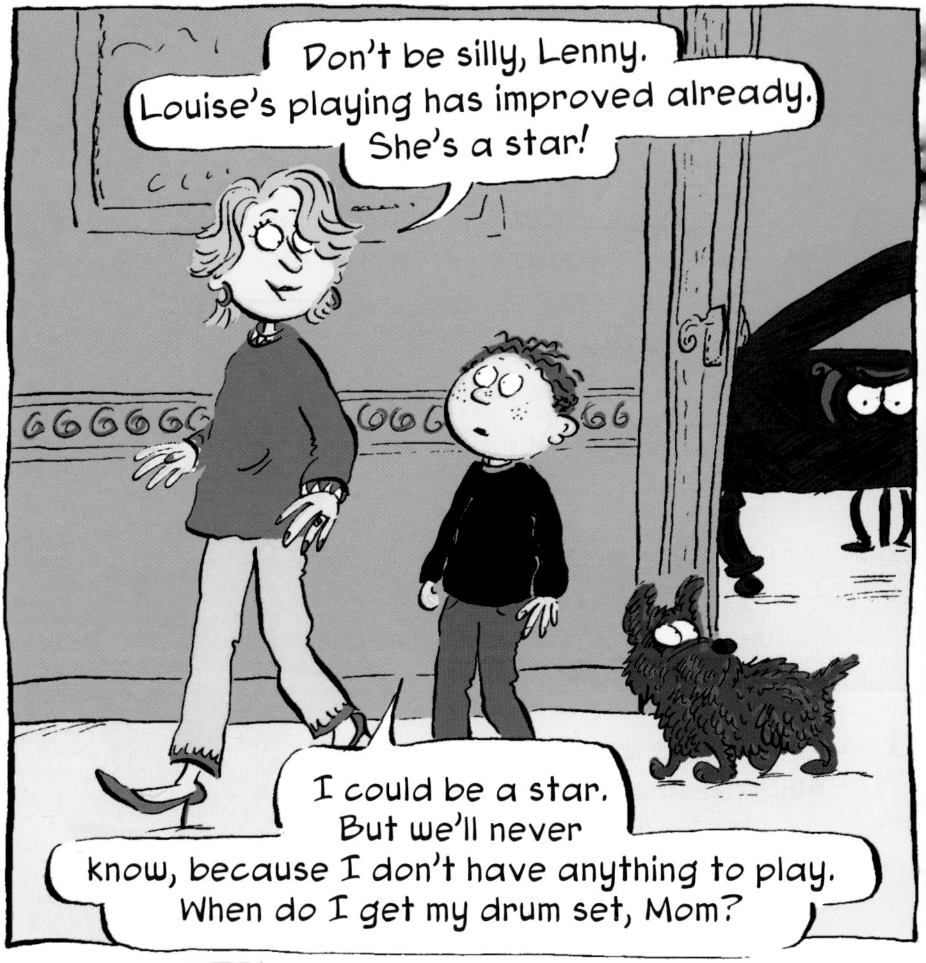
Don't be silly, Lenny. Louise's playing has improved already. She's a star!
I could be a star. But we'll never know, because I don't have anything to play. When do I get my drum set, Mom?

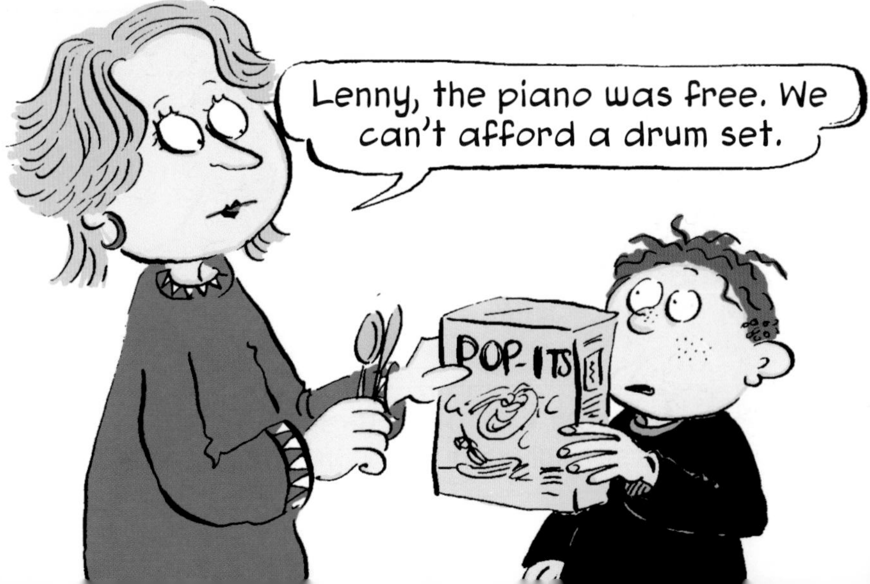
Lenny, the piano was free. We can't afford a drum set.
POP-ITS

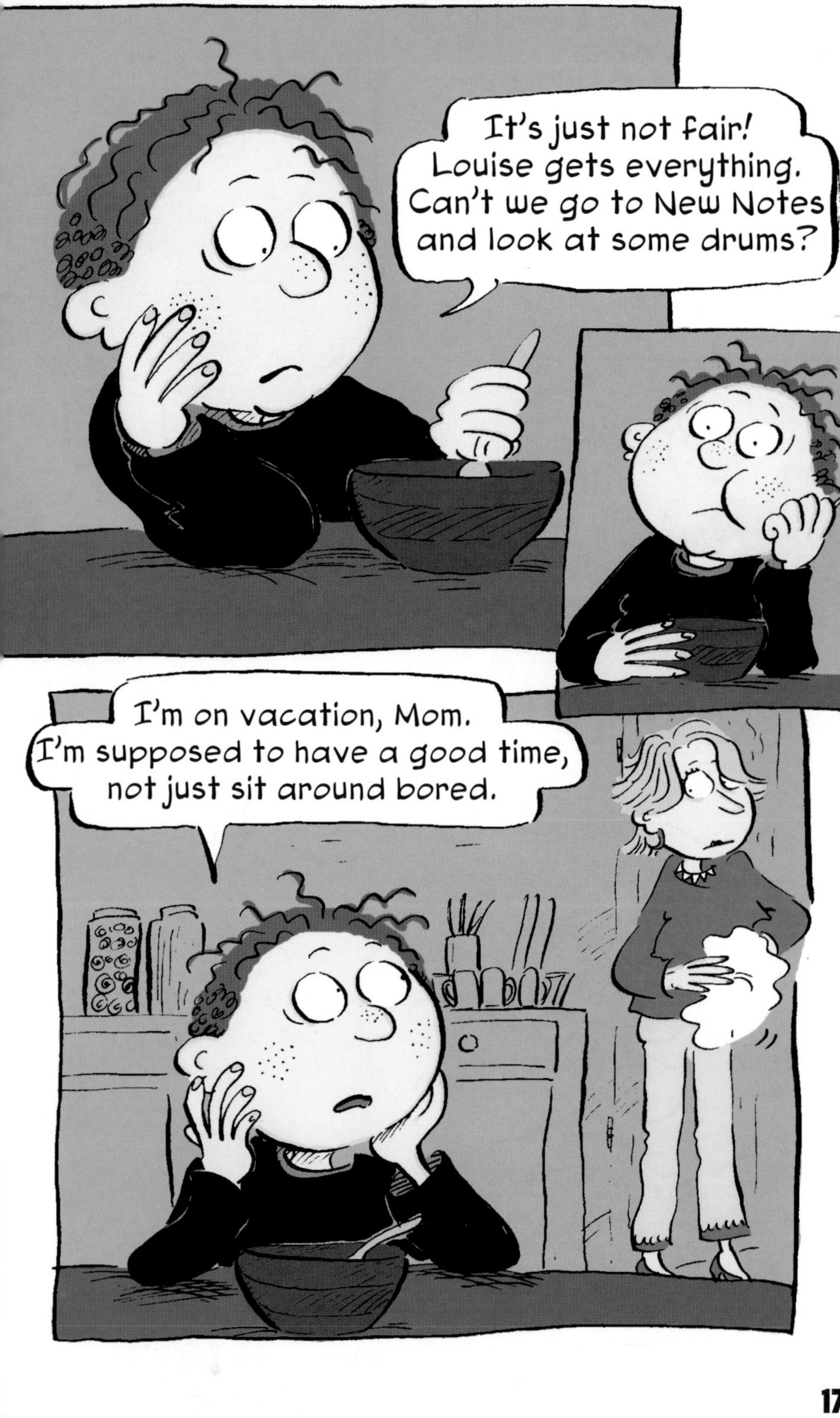
It's just not fair! Louise gets everything. Can't we go to New Notes and look at some drums?
I'm on vacation, Mom. I'm supposed to have a good time, not just sit around bored.

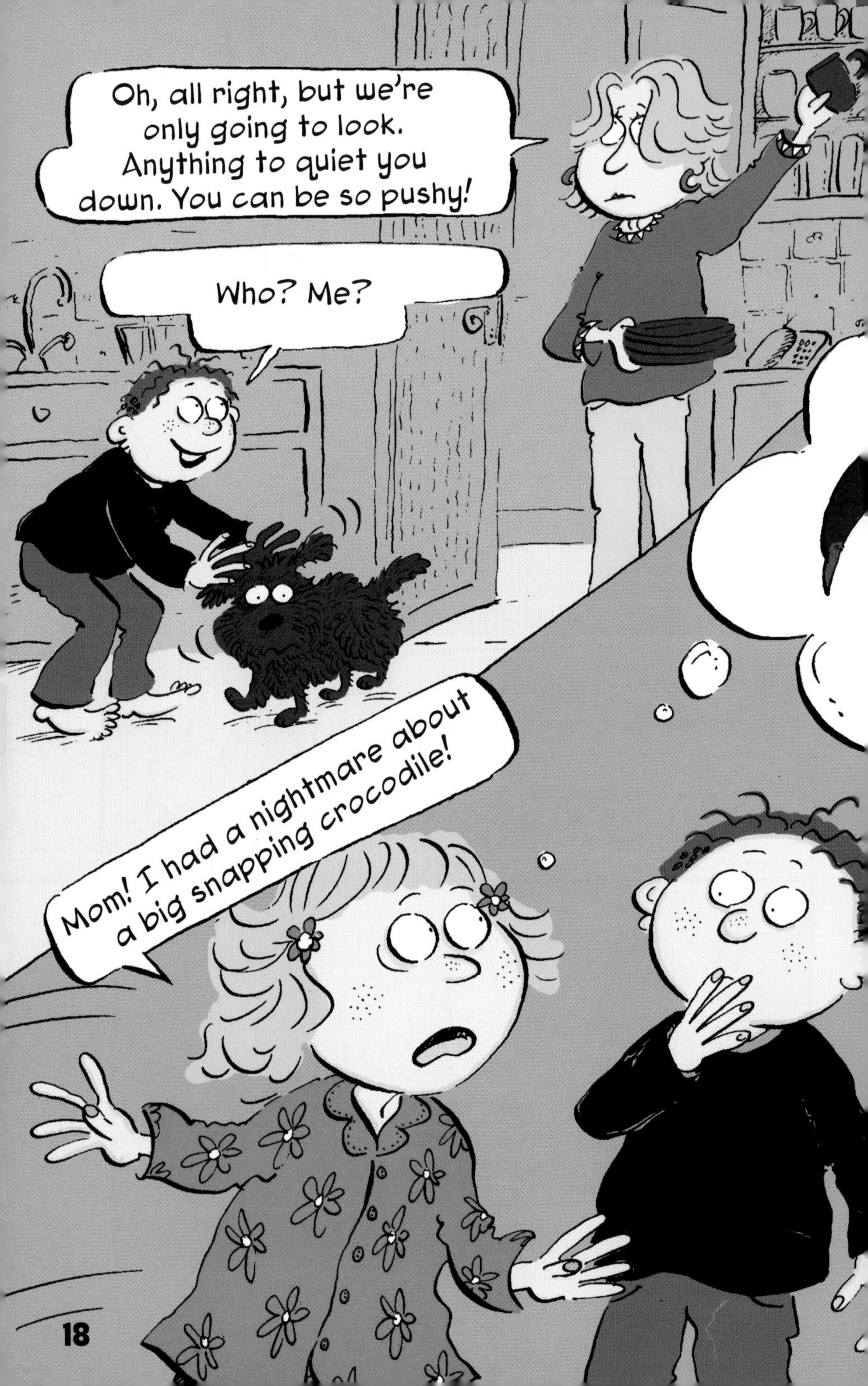

Oh, all right, but we're only going to look. Anything to quiet you down. You can be so pushy!
Who? Me?
Mom! I had a nightmare about a big snapping crocodile!

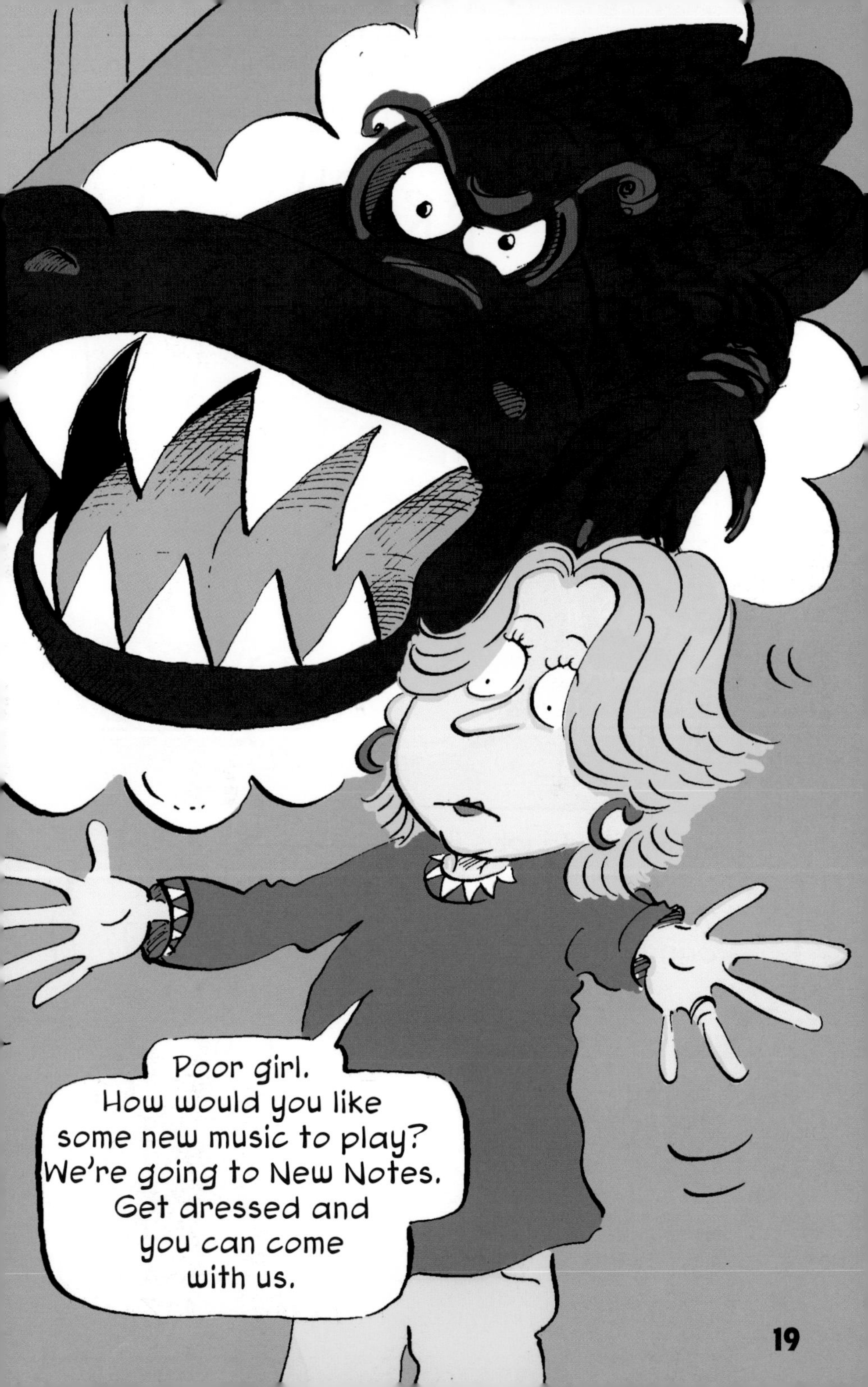
Poor girl. How would you like some new music to play? We're going to New Notes. Get dressed and you can come with us.

Lenny ran all the way to New Notes. He played some cool drums. They were shiny and loud.

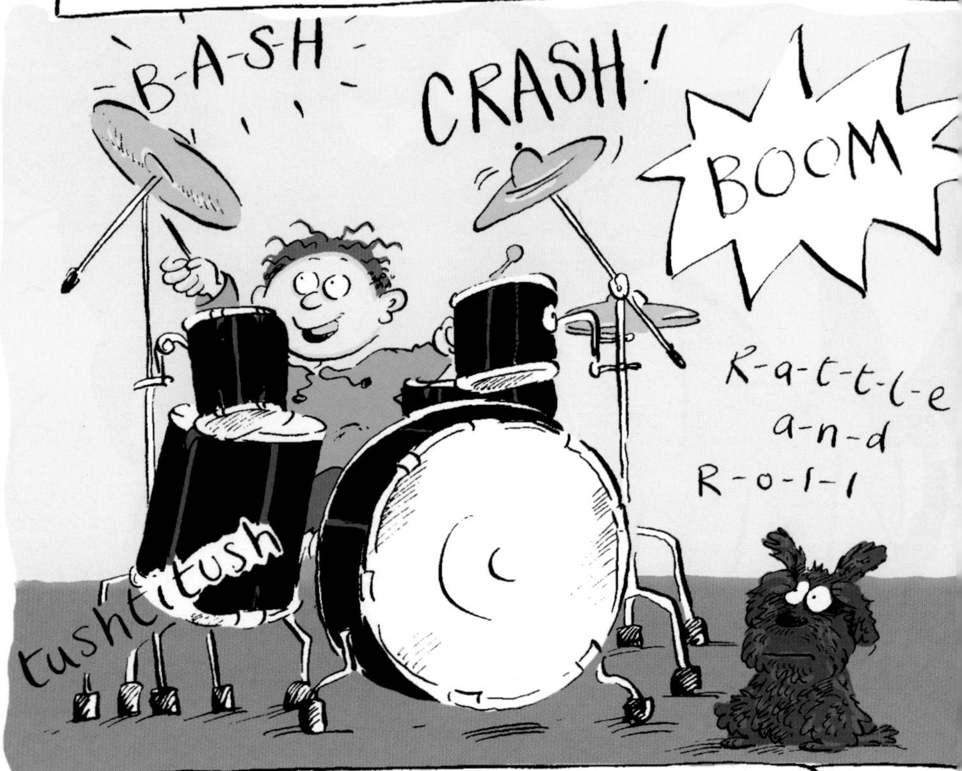
B-A-S-H
CRASH!
BOOM
R-a-t-t-l-e a-n-d R-o-l-l
tush tush

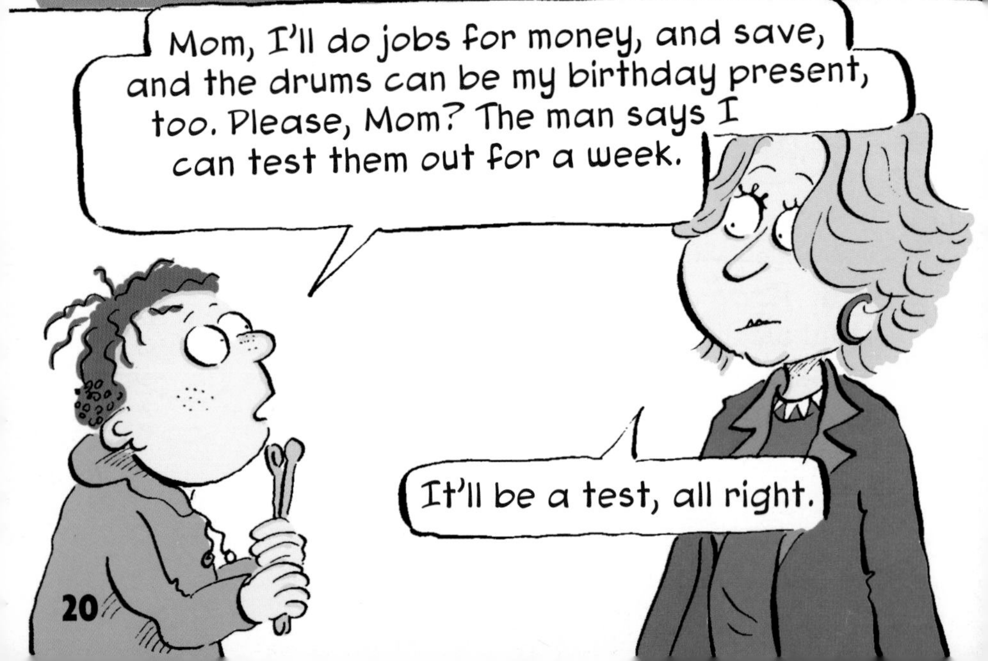
Mom, I'll do jobs for money, and save, and the drums can be my birthday present, too. Please, Mom? The man says I can test them out for a week.
It'll be a test, all right.

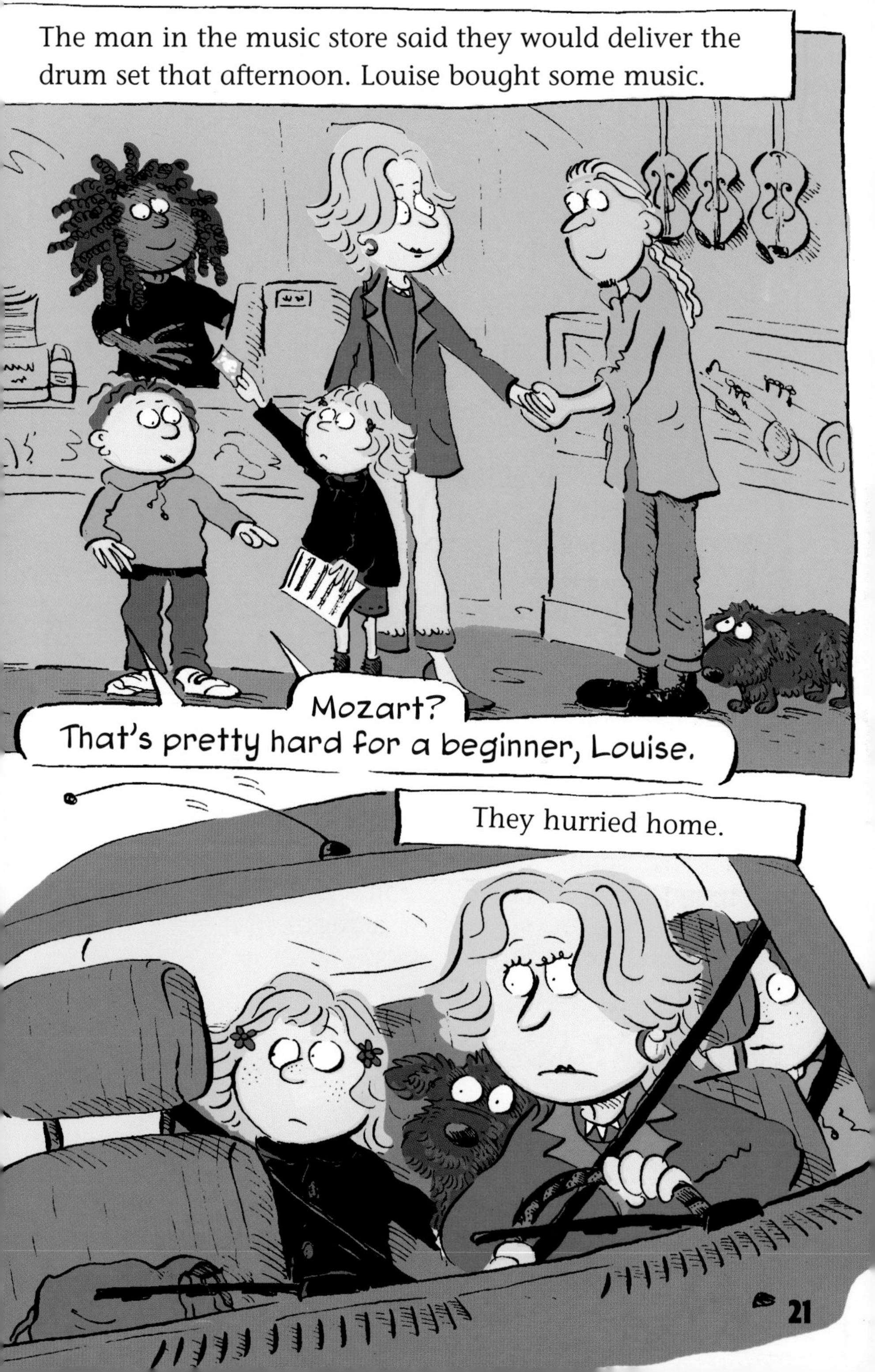
The man in the music store said they would deliver the drum set that afternoon. Louise bought some music.
Mozart?
That's pretty hard for a beginner, Louise.
They hurried home.

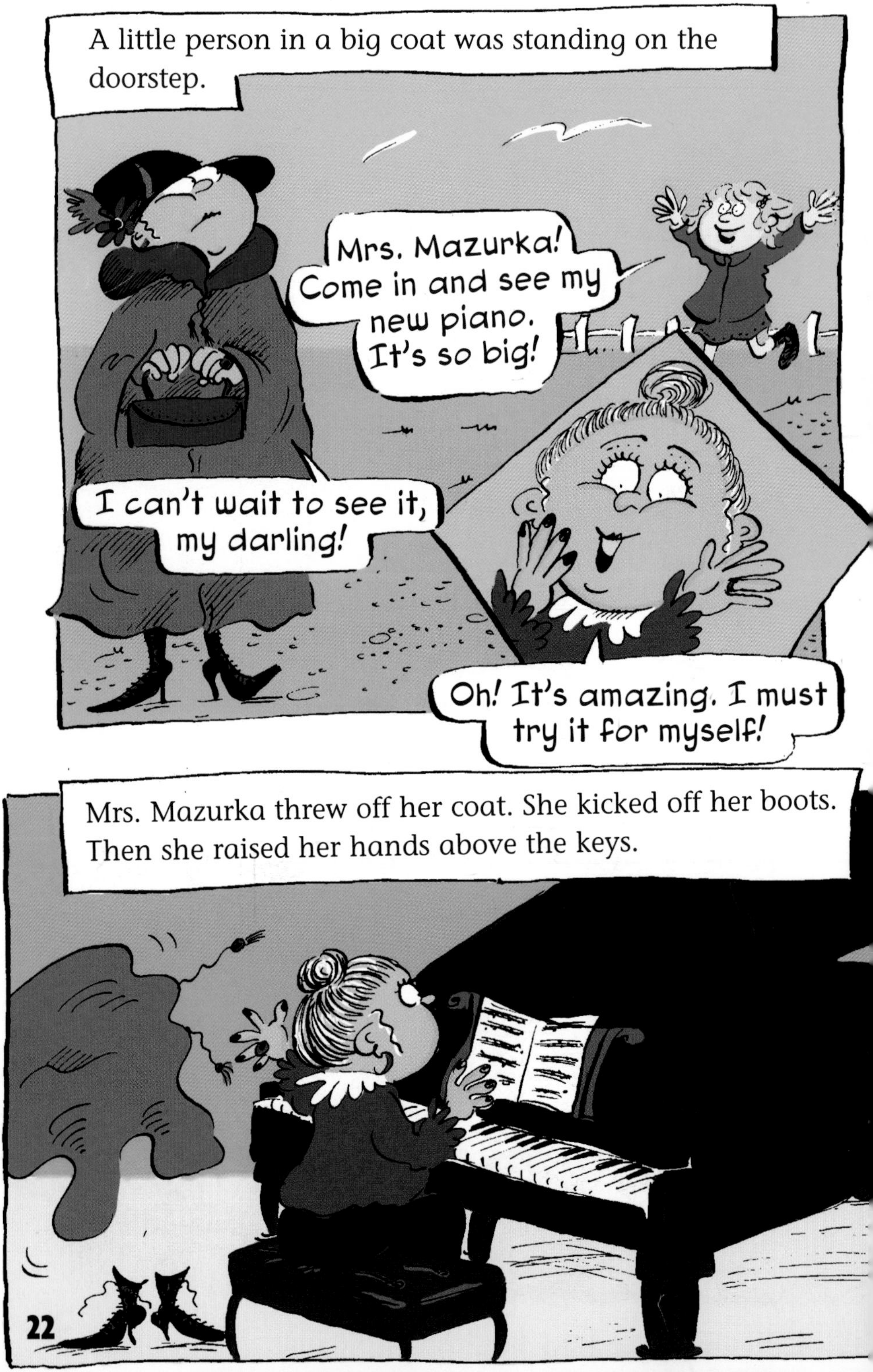
A little person in a big coat was standing on the doorstep.
Mrs. Mazurka! Come in and see my new piano. It's so big!
I can't wait to see it, my darling!
Oh! It's amazing. I must try it for myself!
Mrs. Mazurka threw off her coat. She kicked off her boots. Then she raised her hands above the keys.

Lenny watched Mrs. Mazurka.

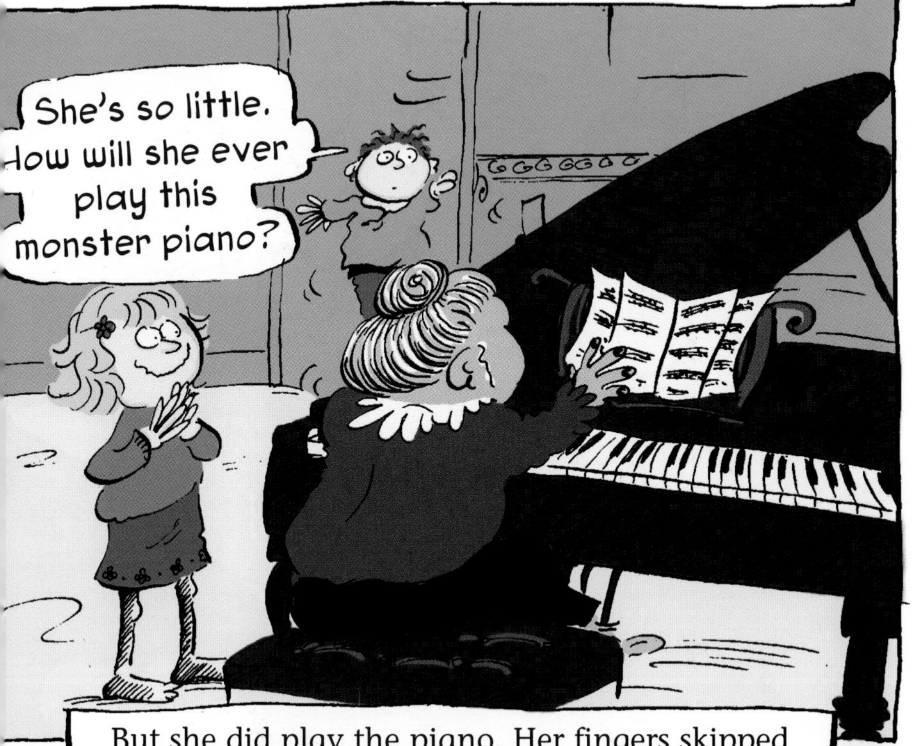
She's so little. How will she ever play this monster piano?

But she did play the piano. Her fingers skipped across the keys.

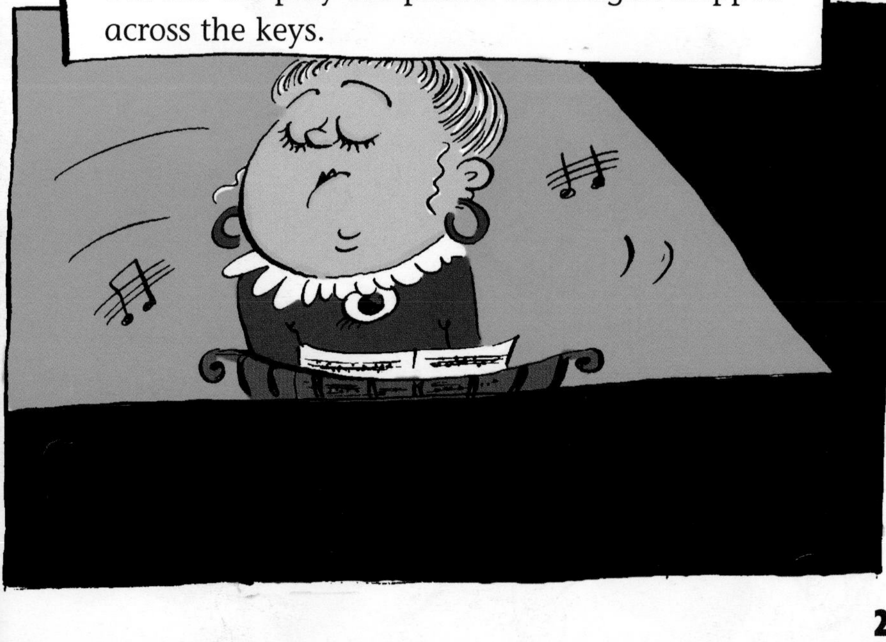

She played wonderful music. It sounded like it was about kings and magicians, heroes and villains, and horses running and planets twirling.

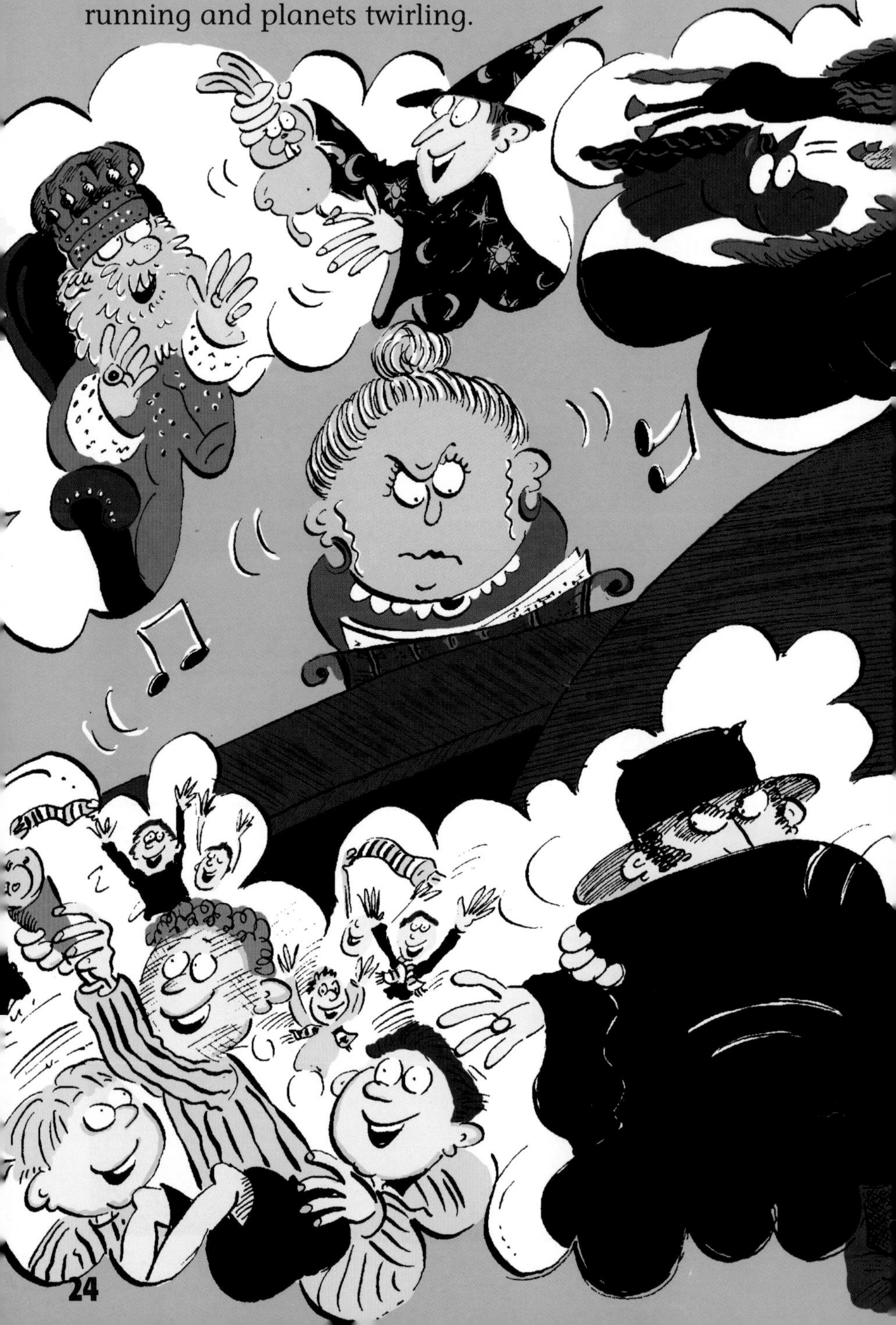

Lenny felt like he was being swept down a river of music, over a waterfall, and out to the ocean.

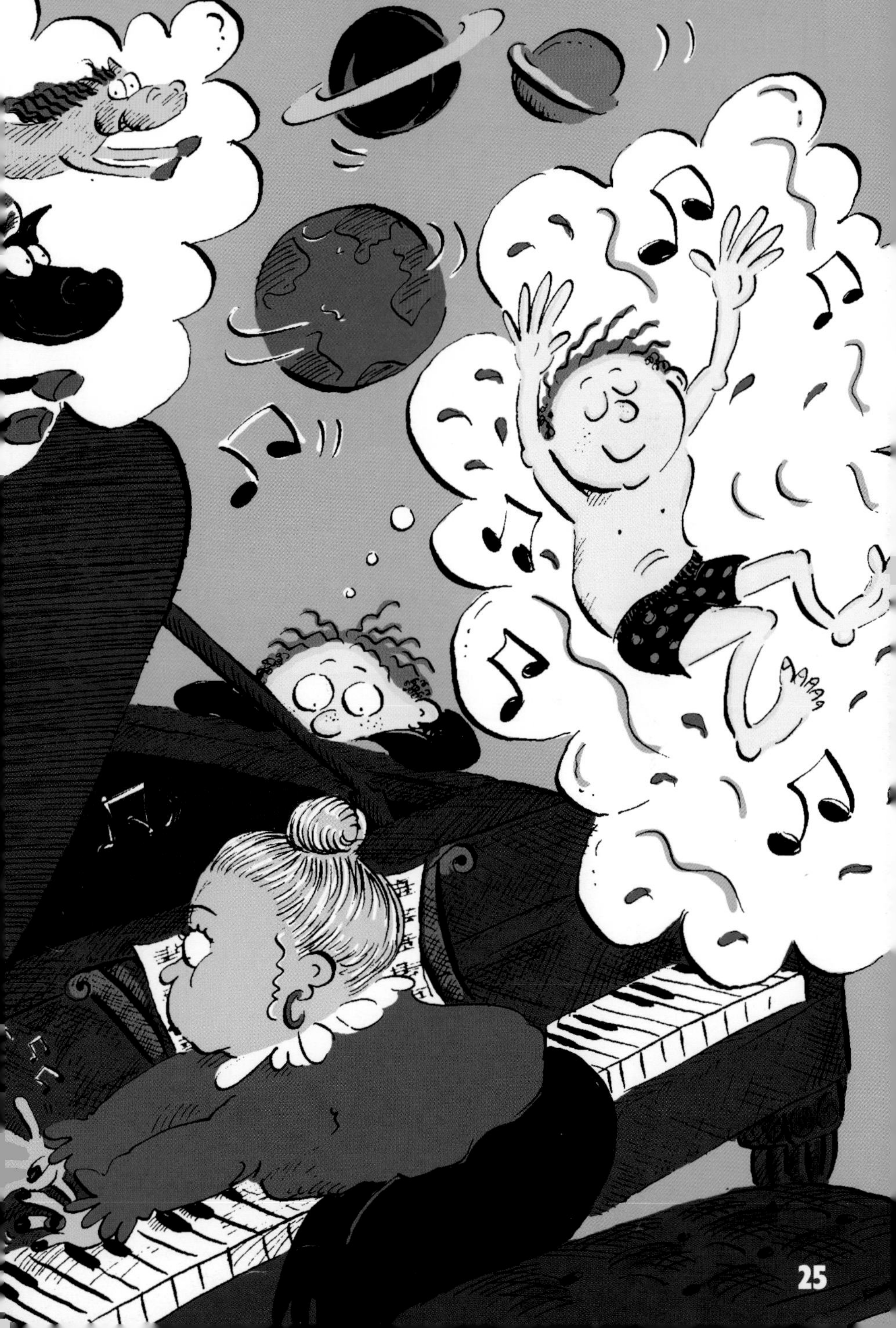

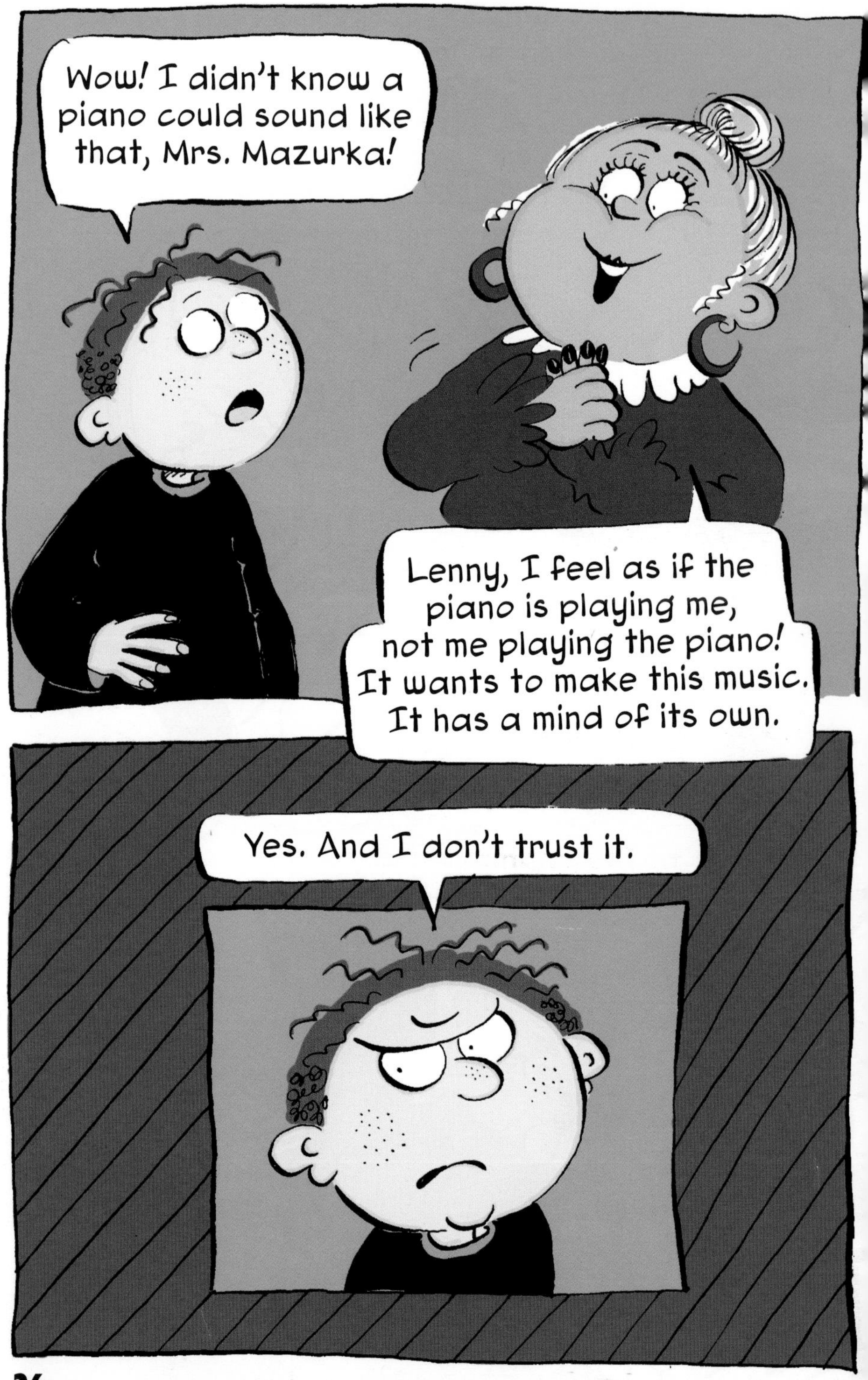
Wow! I didn't know a piano could sound like that, Mrs. Mazurka!
Lenny, I feel as if the piano is playing me, not me playing the piano! It wants to make this music. It has a mind of its own.
Yes. And I don't trust it.

Chapter Five

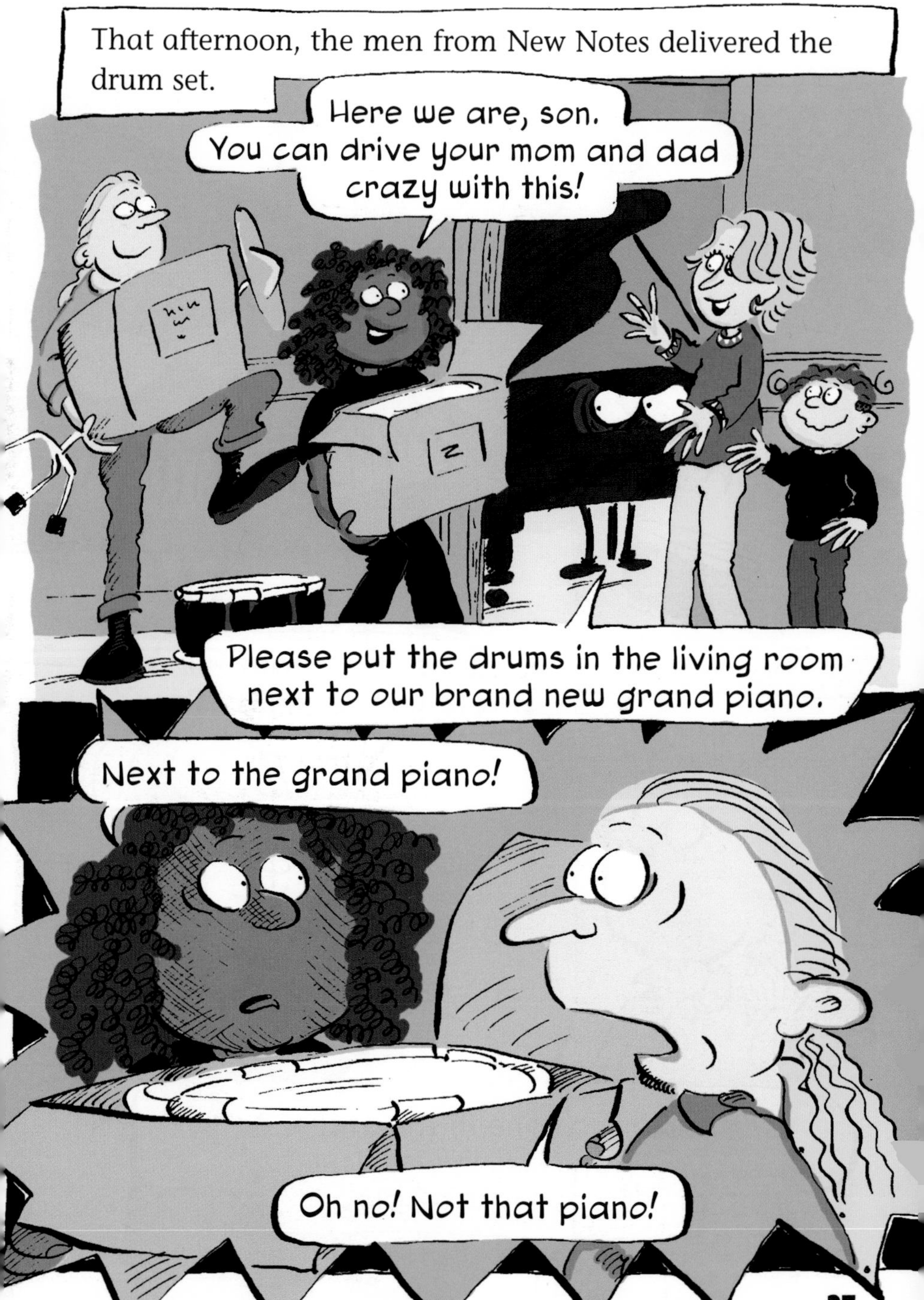
That afternoon, the men from New Notes delivered the drum set.
Here we are, son. You can drive your mom and dad crazy with this!
Please put the drums in the living room next to our brand new grand piano.
Next to the grand piano!
Oh no! Not that piano!

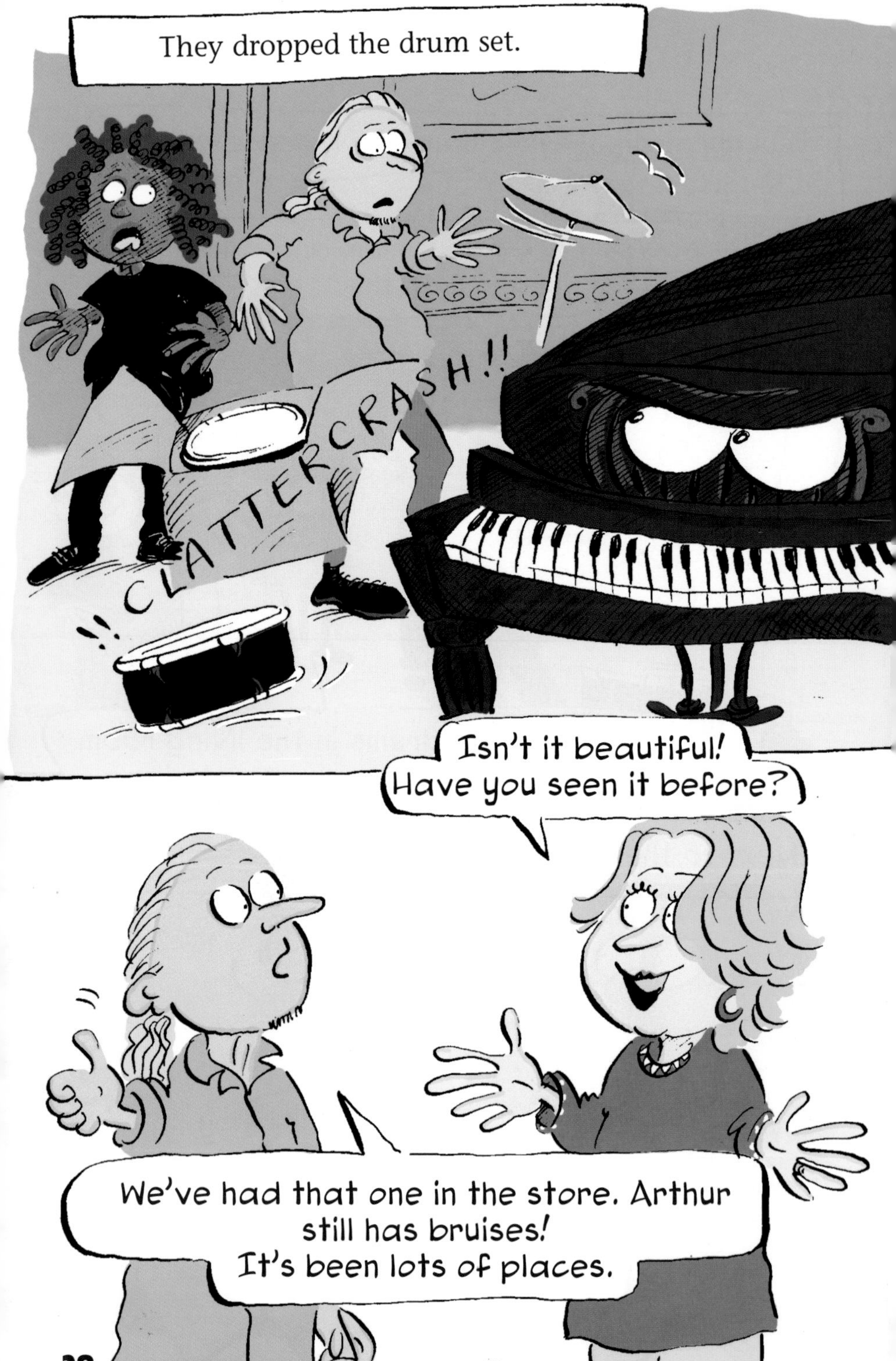
They dropped the drum set.
CLATTERCRASH!!
Isn't it beautiful! Have you seen it before?
We've had that one in the store. Arthur still has bruises! It's been lots of places.

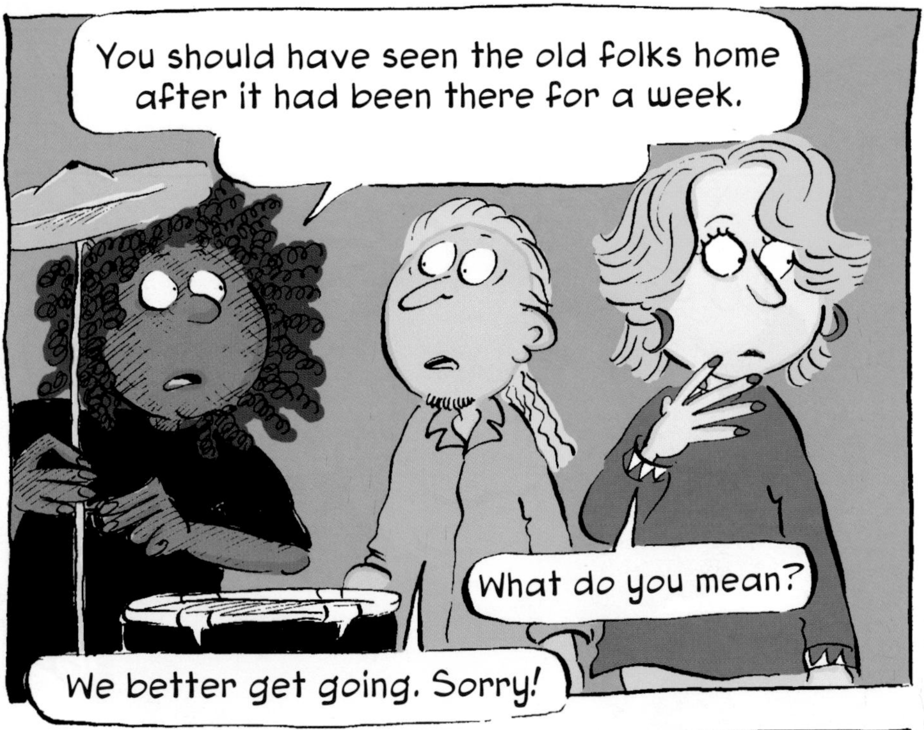
You should have seen the old folks home after it had been there for a week.
What do you mean?
We better get going. Sorry!

The men left quickly. Mom began polishing the piano. Lenny rushed over to his new drum set.

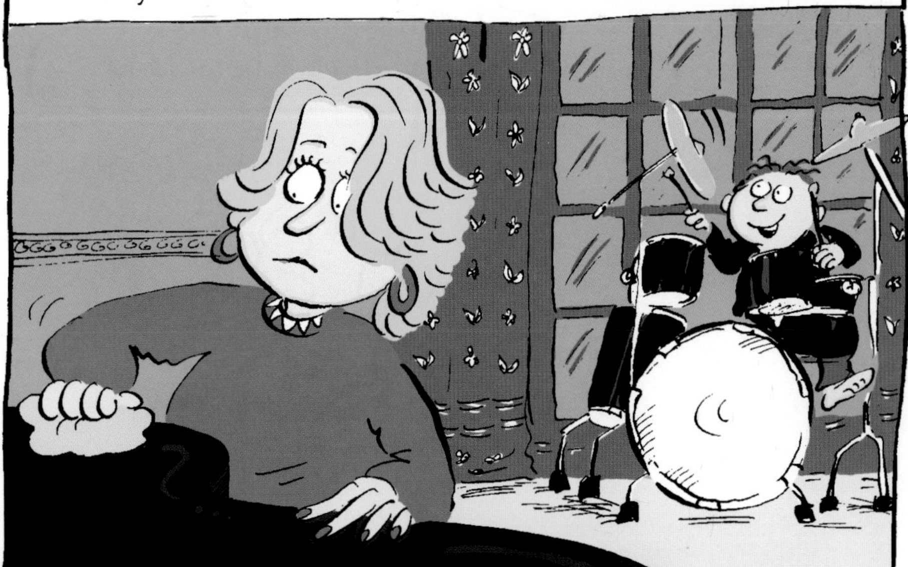

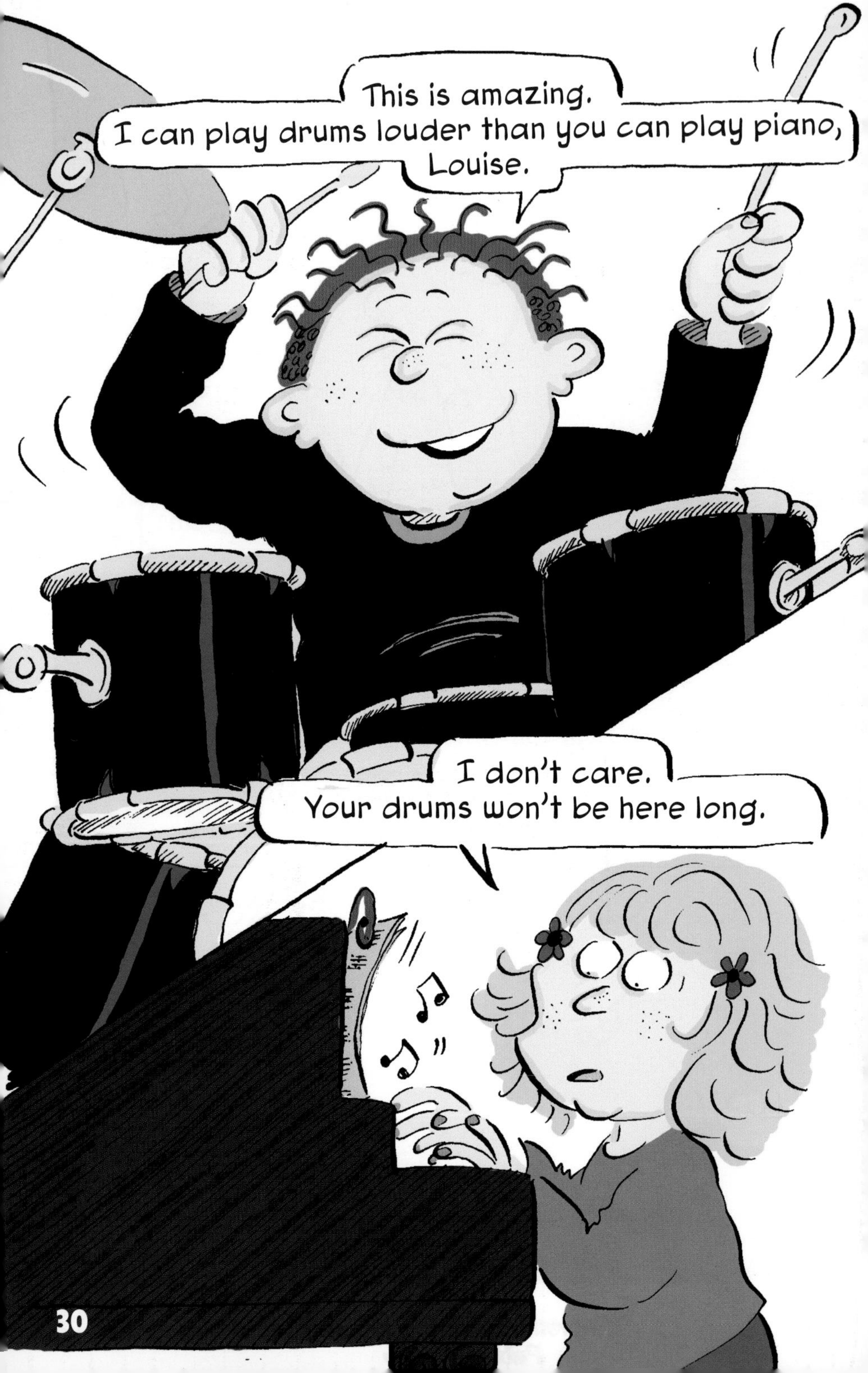
This is amazing.
I can play drums louder than you can play piano, Louise.
I don't care.
Your drums won't be here long.

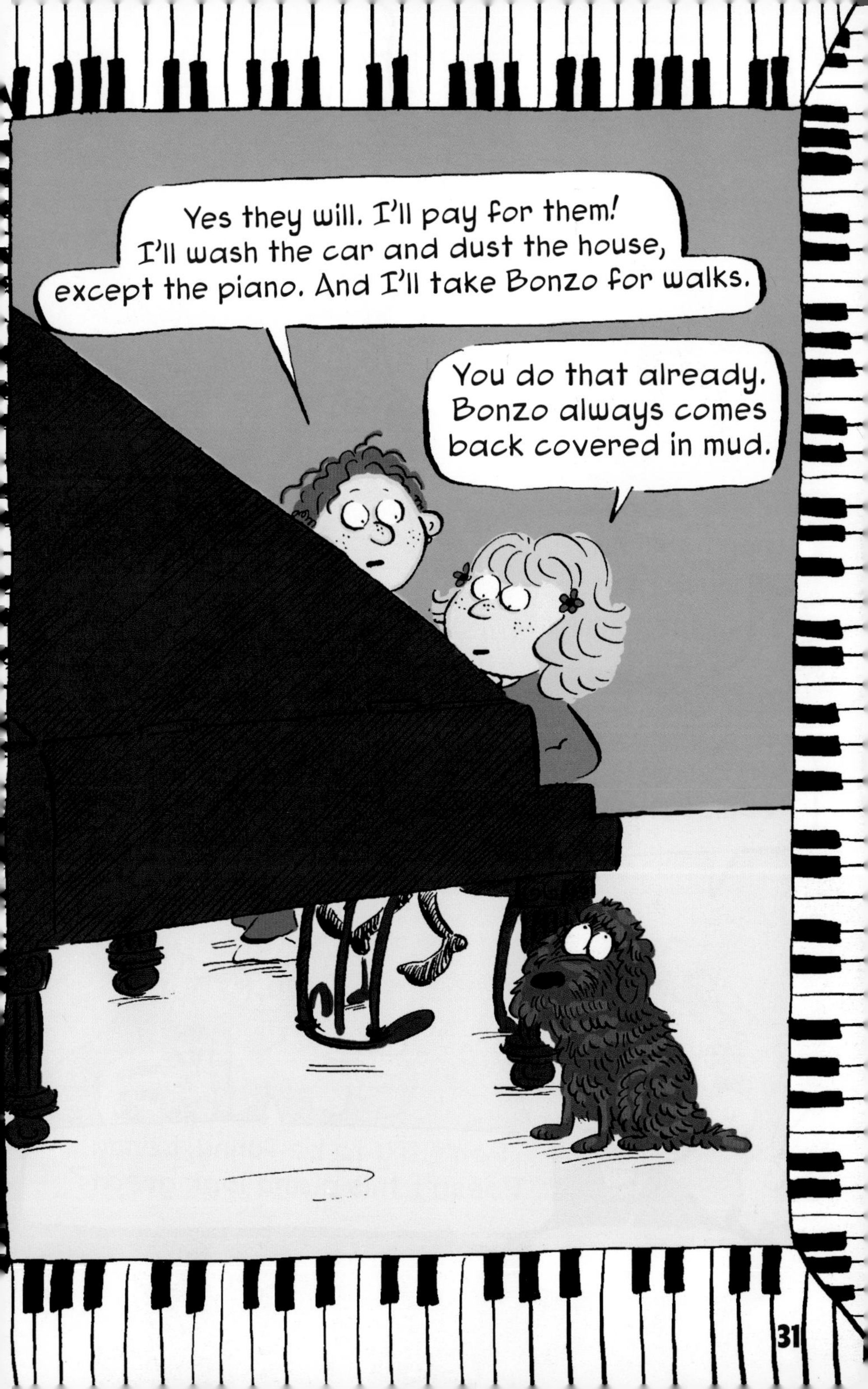
Yes they will. I'll pay for them! I'll wash the car and dust the house, except the piano. And I'll take Bonzo for walks.
You do that already. Bonzo always comes back covered in mud.

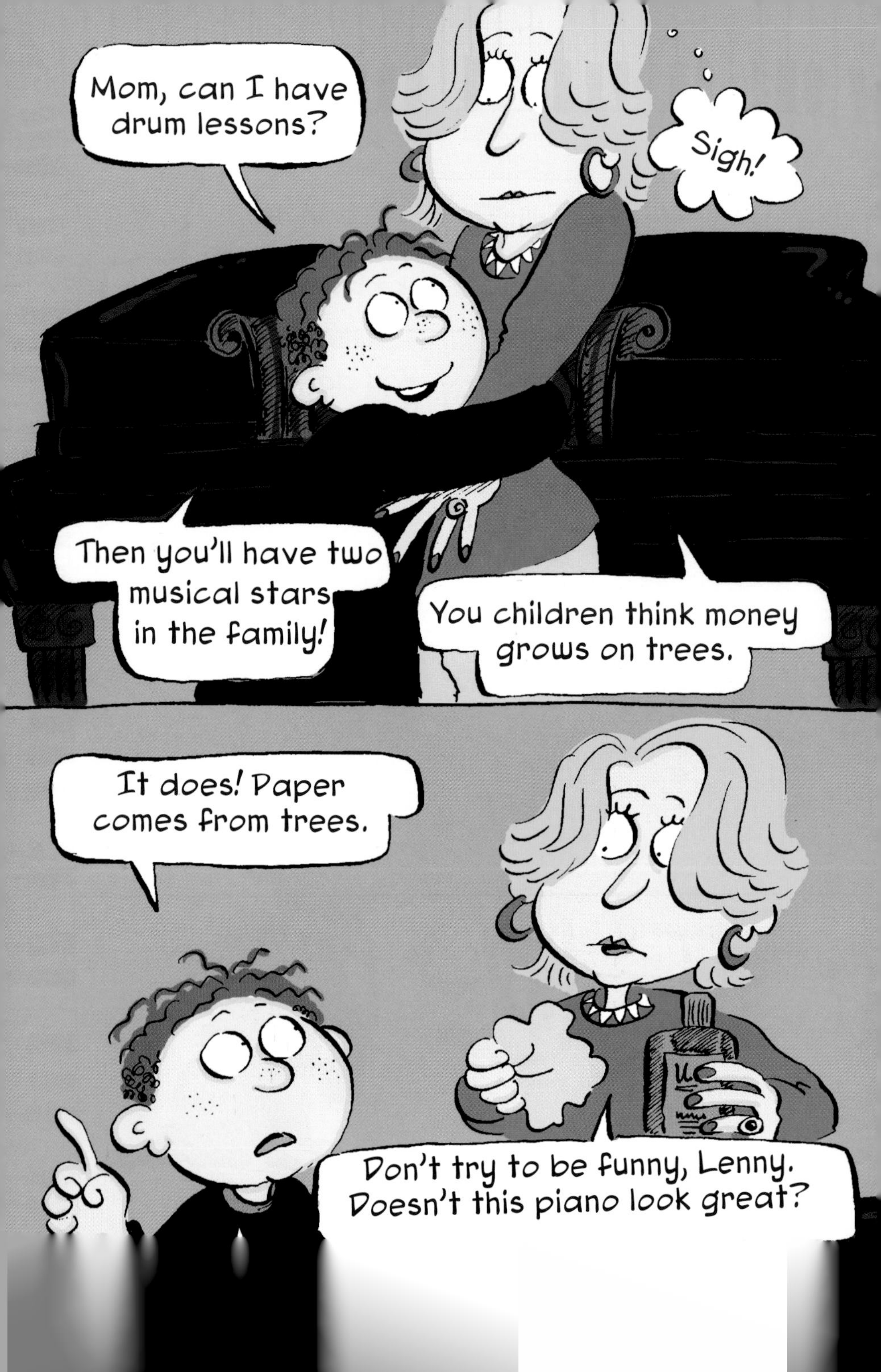
Mom, can I have drum lessons?
Sigh!
Then you'll have two musical stars in the family!
You children think money grows on trees.
It does! Paper comes from trees.
Don't try to be funny, Lenny. Doesn't this piano look great?

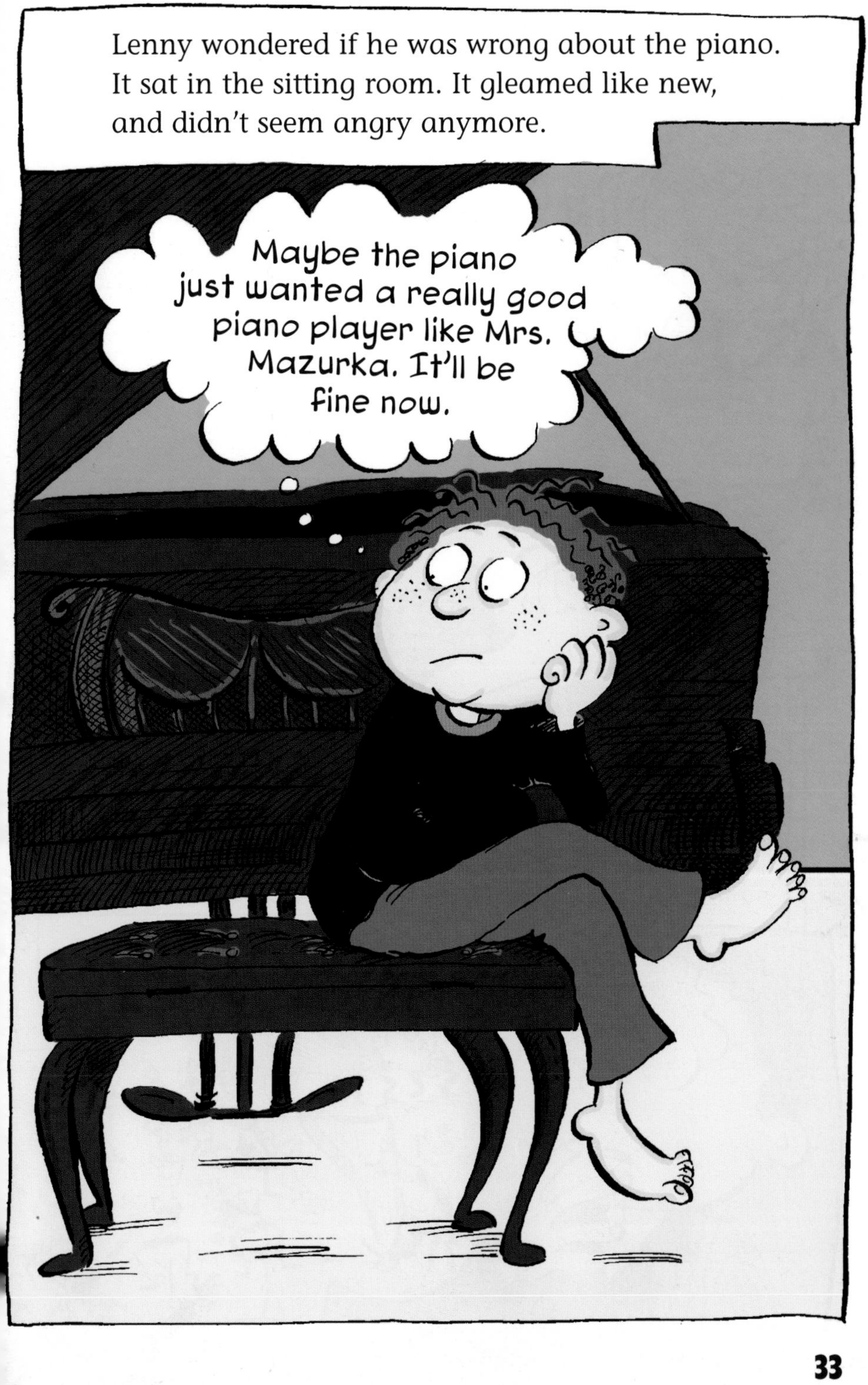
Lenny wondered if he was wrong about the piano. It sat in the sitting room. It gleamed like new, and didn't seem angry anymore.
Maybe the piano just wanted a really good piano player like Mrs. Mazurka. It'll be fine now.

Chapter Six

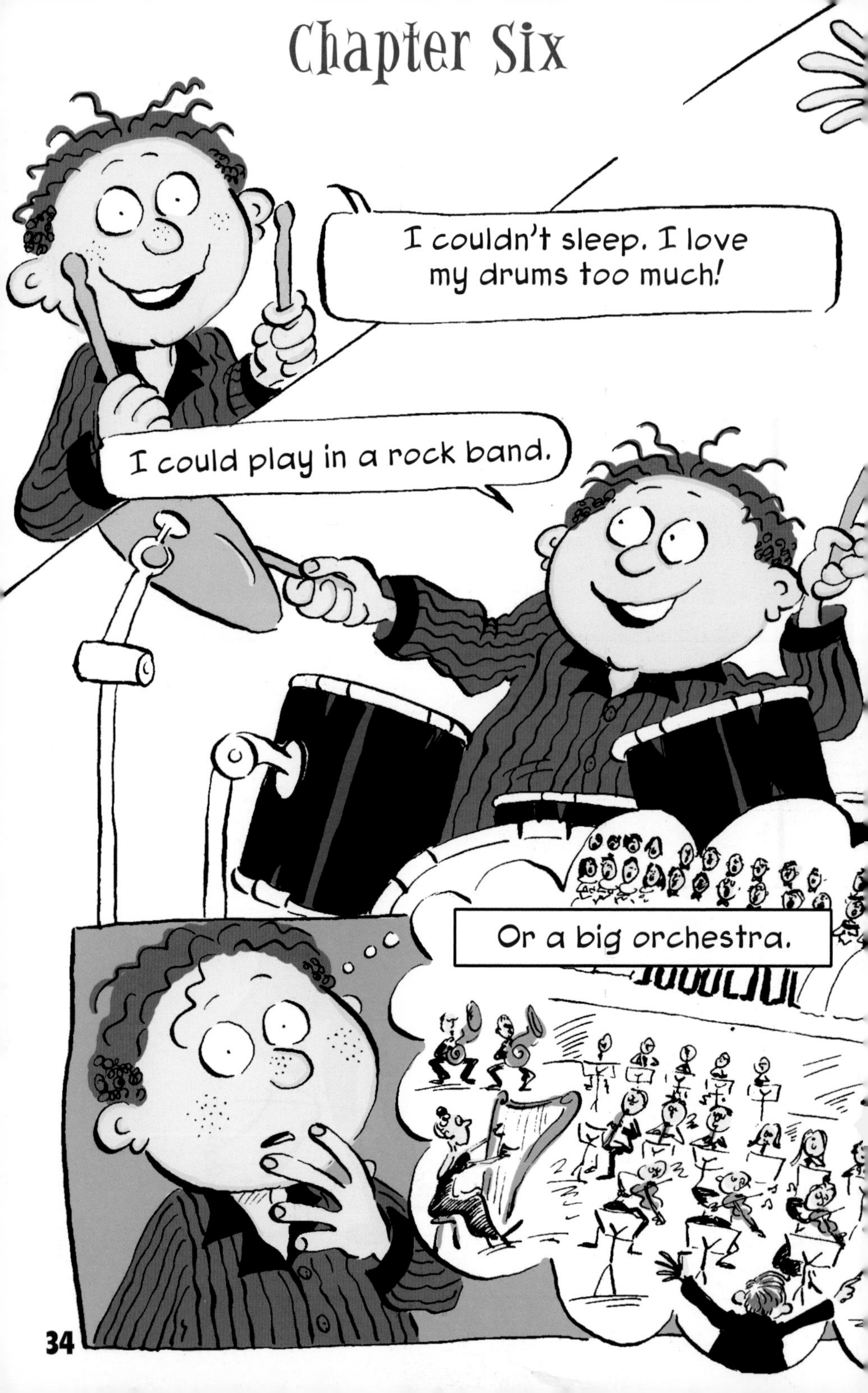
I couldn't sleep. I love my drums too much!
I could play in a rock band.
Or a big orchestra.

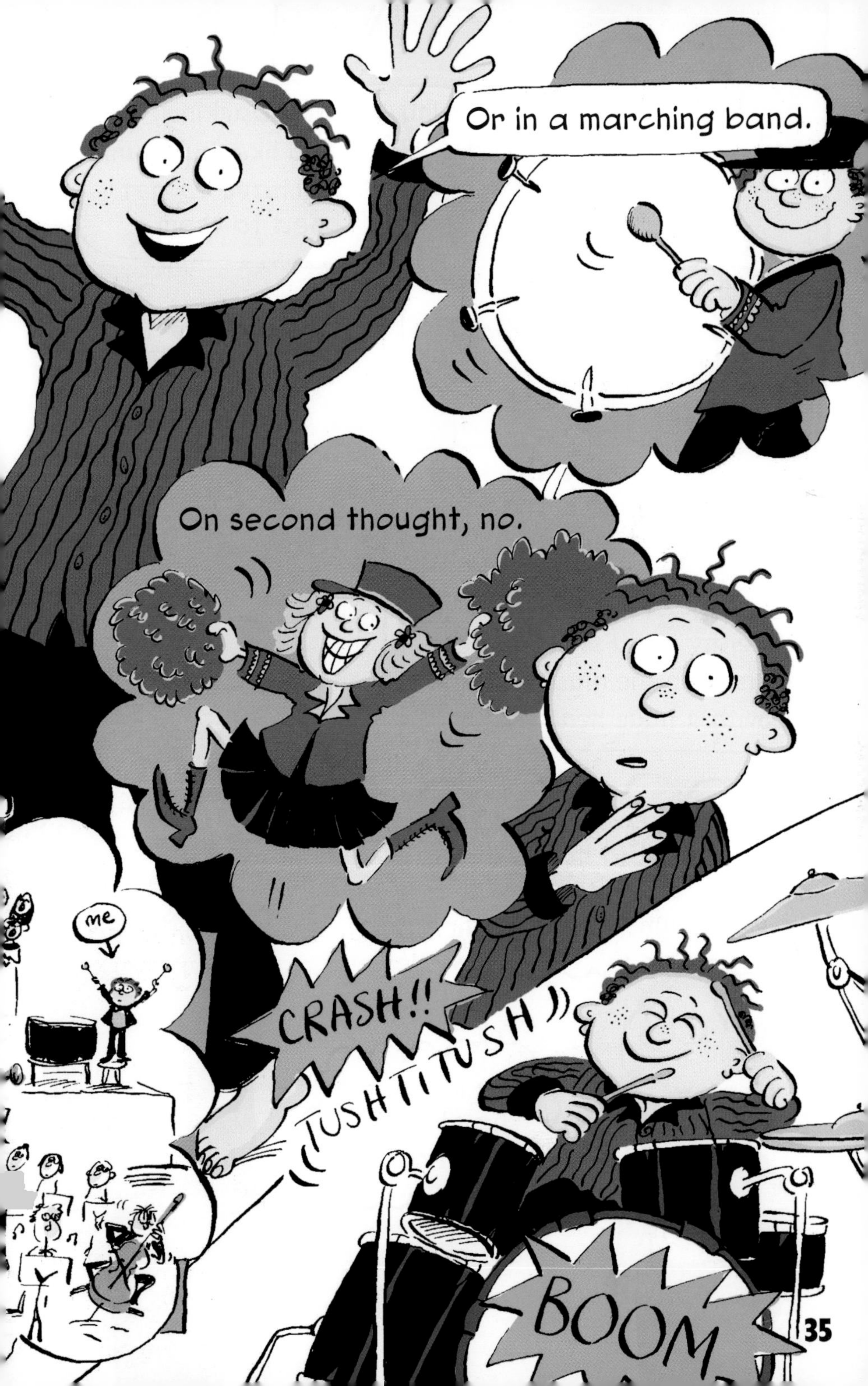
Or in a marching band.
On second thought, no.
me
CRASH!!
TUSH TI TUSH
BOOM

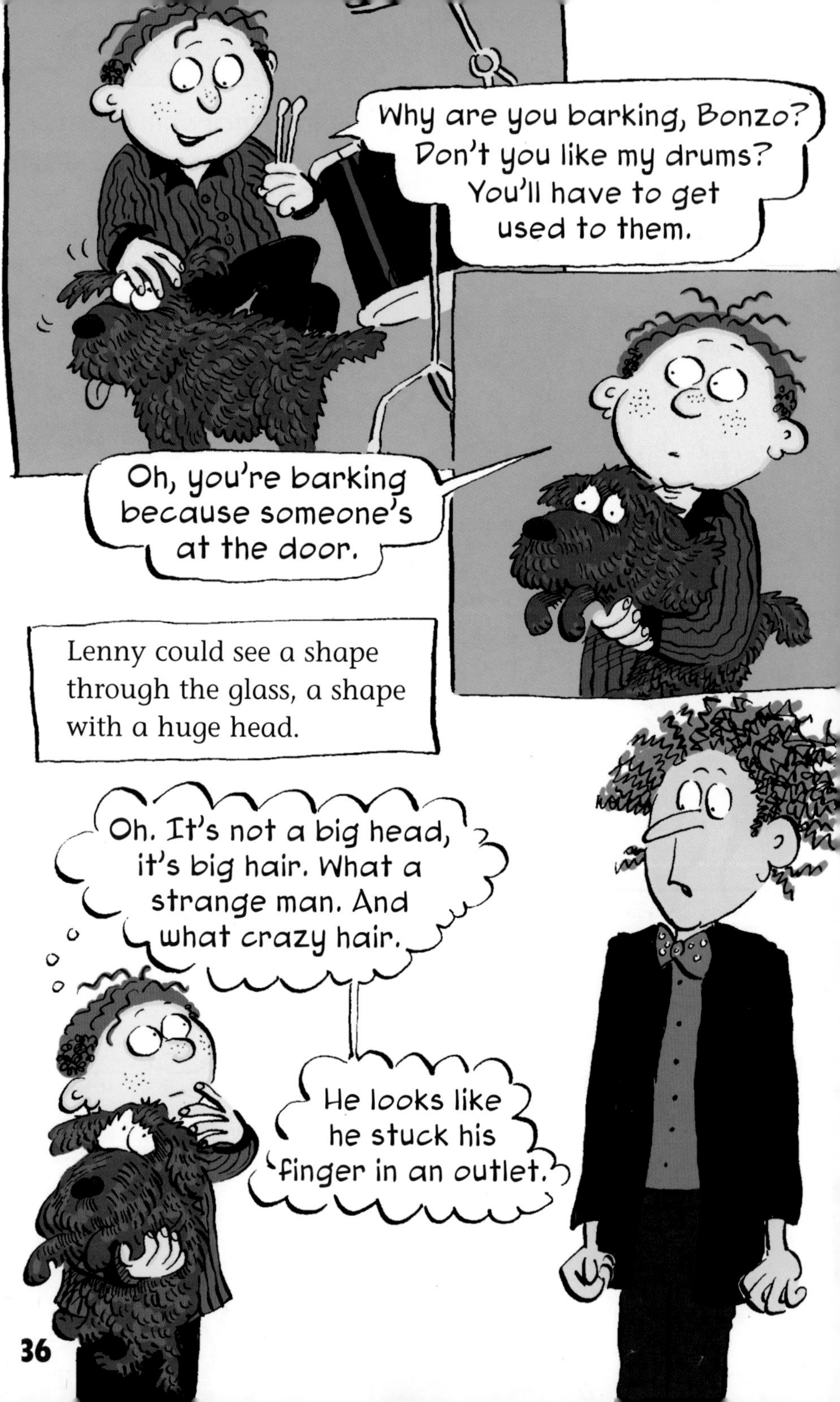
Why are you barking, Bonzo? Don't you like my drums? You'll have to get used to them.
Oh, you're barking because someone's at the door.
Lenny could see a shape through the glass, a shape with a huge head.
Oh. It's not a big head, it's big hair. What a strange man. And what crazy hair.
He looks like he stuck his finger in an outlet.

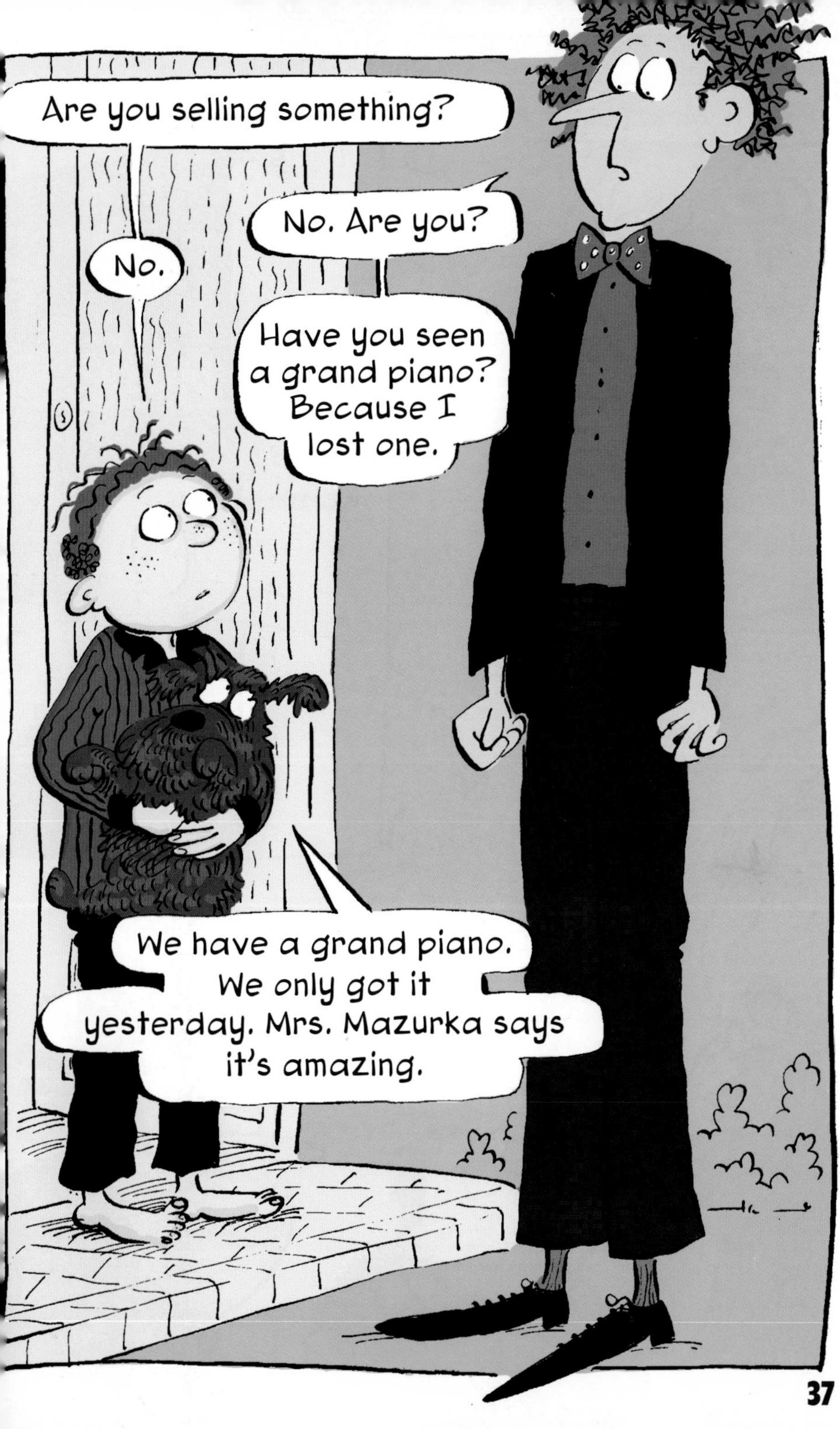
Are you selling something?
No.
No. Are you?
Have you seen a grand piano? Because I lost one.
We have a grand piano. We only got it yesterday. Mrs. Mazurka says it's amazing.

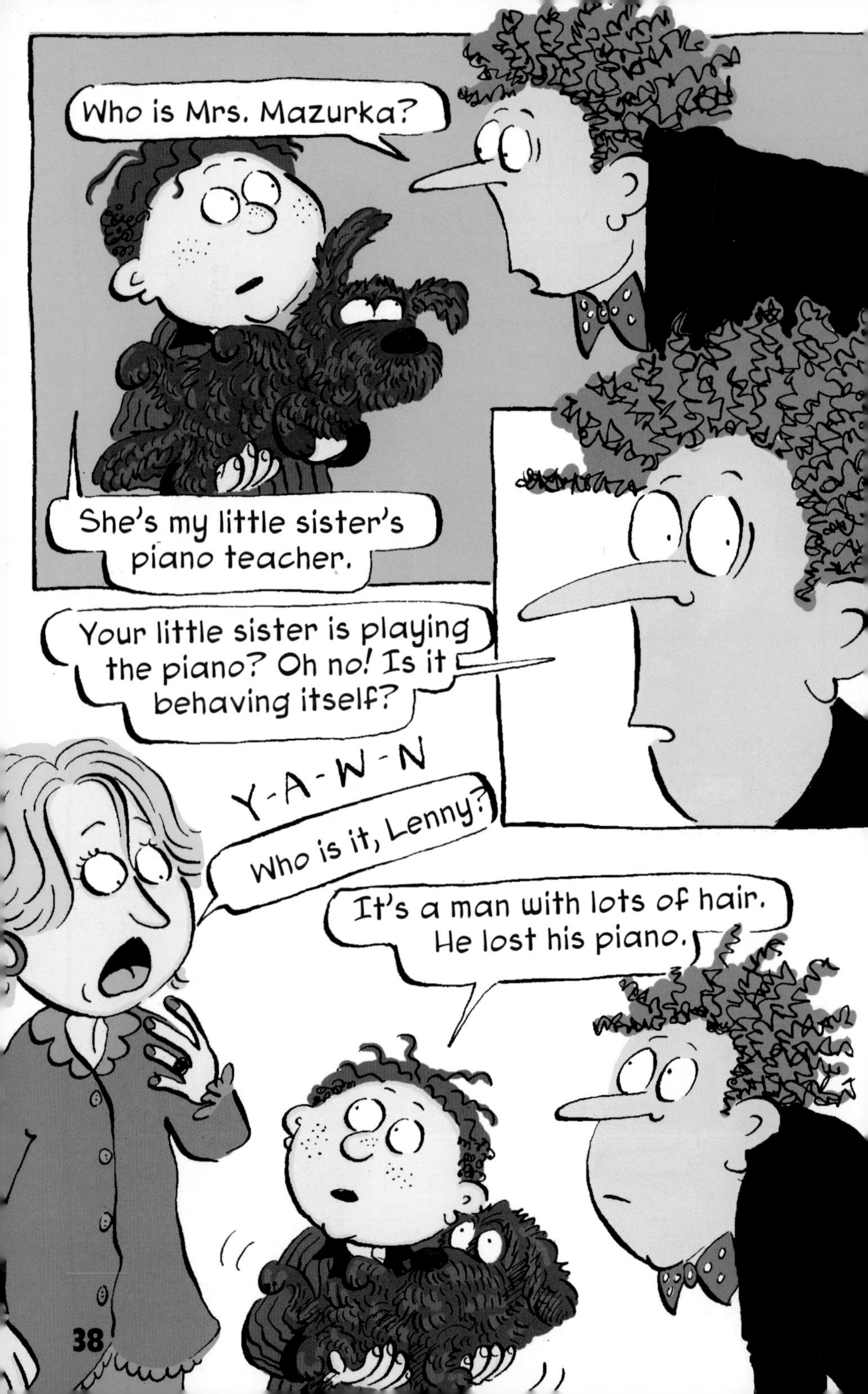
Who is Mrs. Mazurka?
She's my little sister's piano teacher.
Your little sister is playing the piano? Oh no! Is it behaving itself?
Y-A-W-N
Who is it, Lenny?
It's a man with lots of hair. He lost his piano.

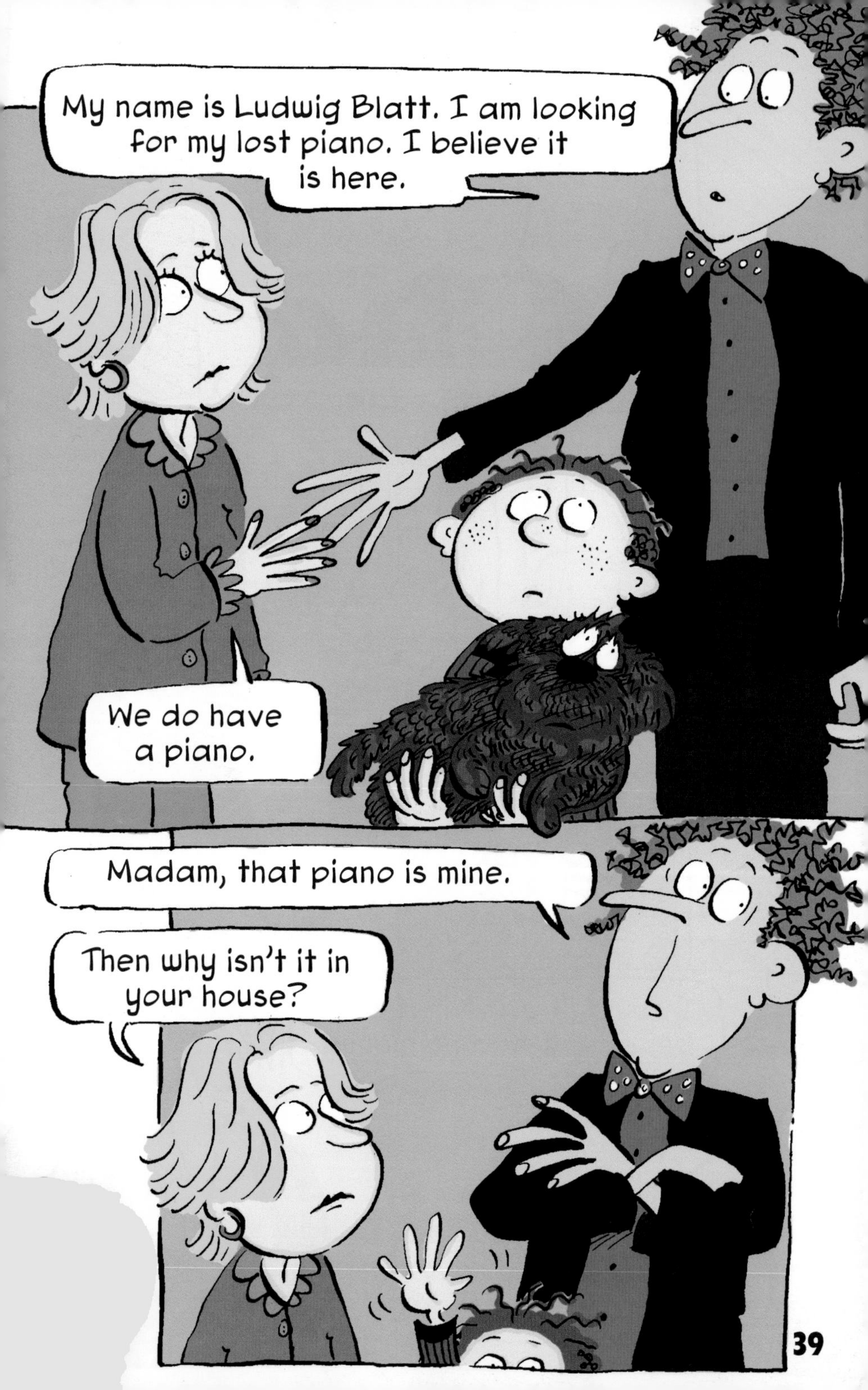
My name is Ludwig Blatt. I am looking for my lost piano. I believe it is here.
We do have a piano.
Madam, that piano is mine.
Then why isn't it in your house?

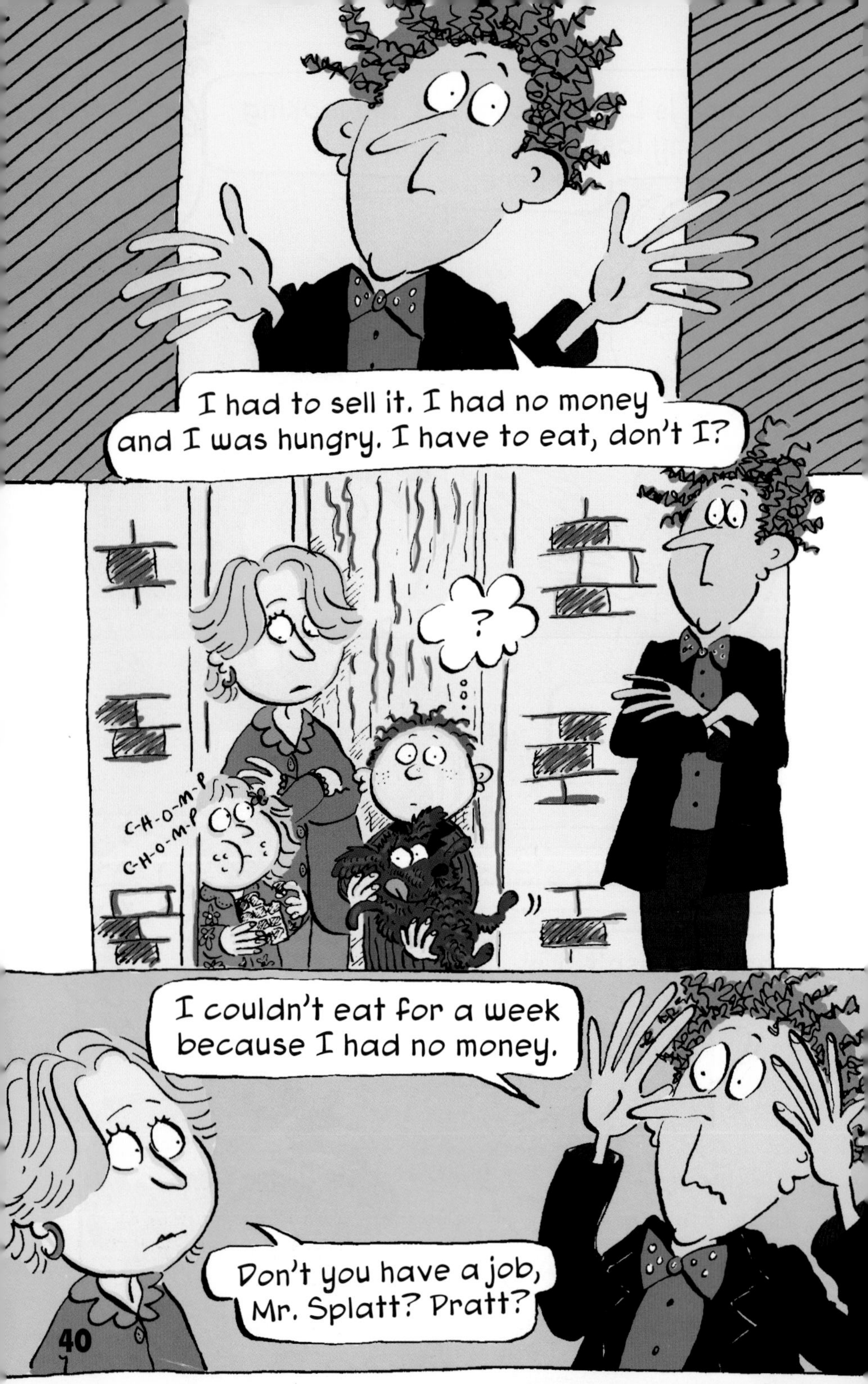
I had to sell it. I had no money and I was hungry. I have to eat, don't I?
?
C-H-O-M-P
C-H-O-M-P
I couldn't eat for a week because I had no money.
Don't you have a job, Mr. Splatt? Pratt?

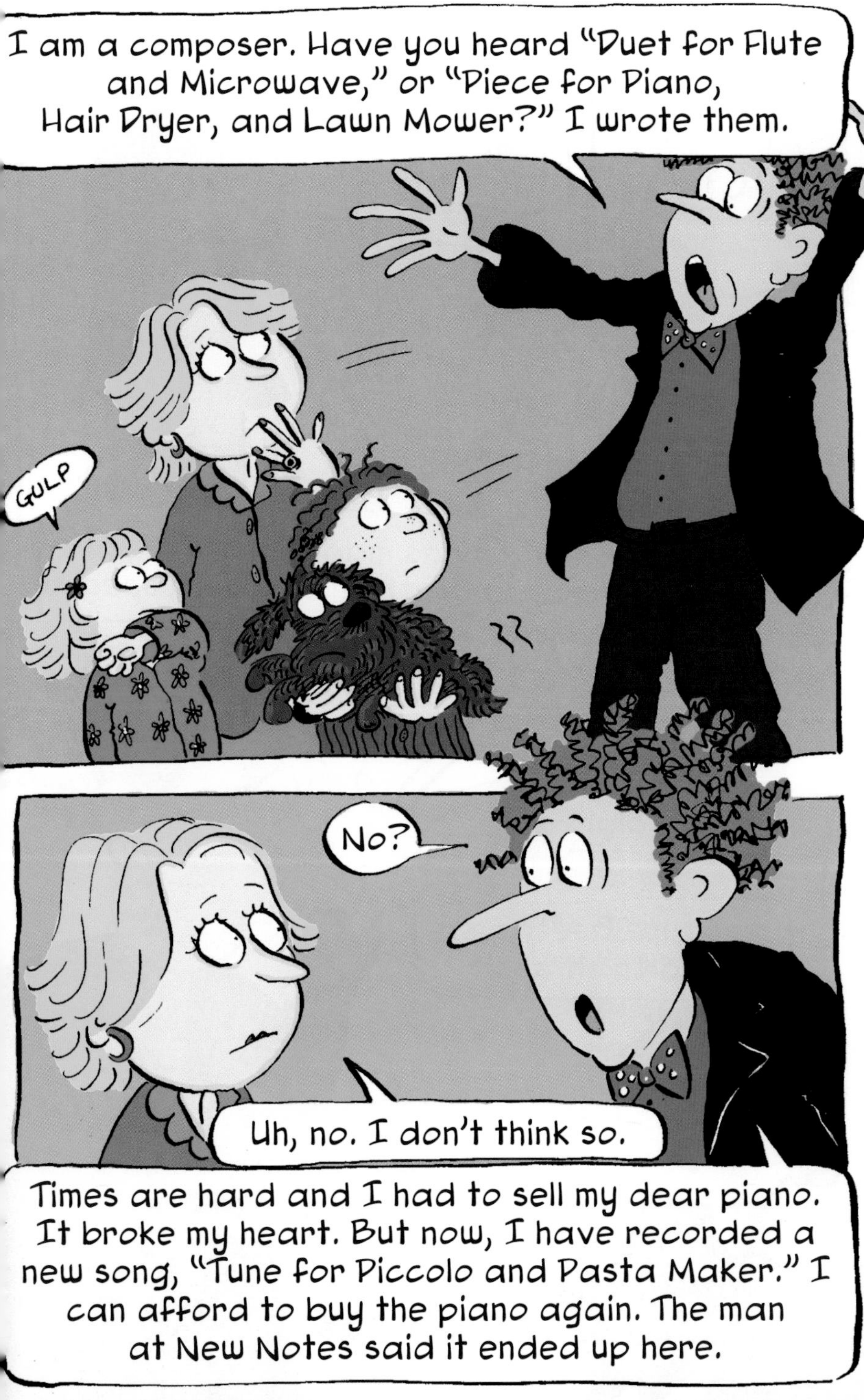
I am a composer. Have you heard "Duet for Flute and Microwave," or "Piece for Piano, Hair Dryer, and Lawn Mower?" I wrote them.
GULP
No?
Uh, no. I don't think so.
Times are hard and I had to sell my dear piano. It broke my heart. But now, I have recorded a new song, "Tune for Piccolo and Pasta Maker." I can afford to buy the piano again. The man at New Notes said it ended up here.

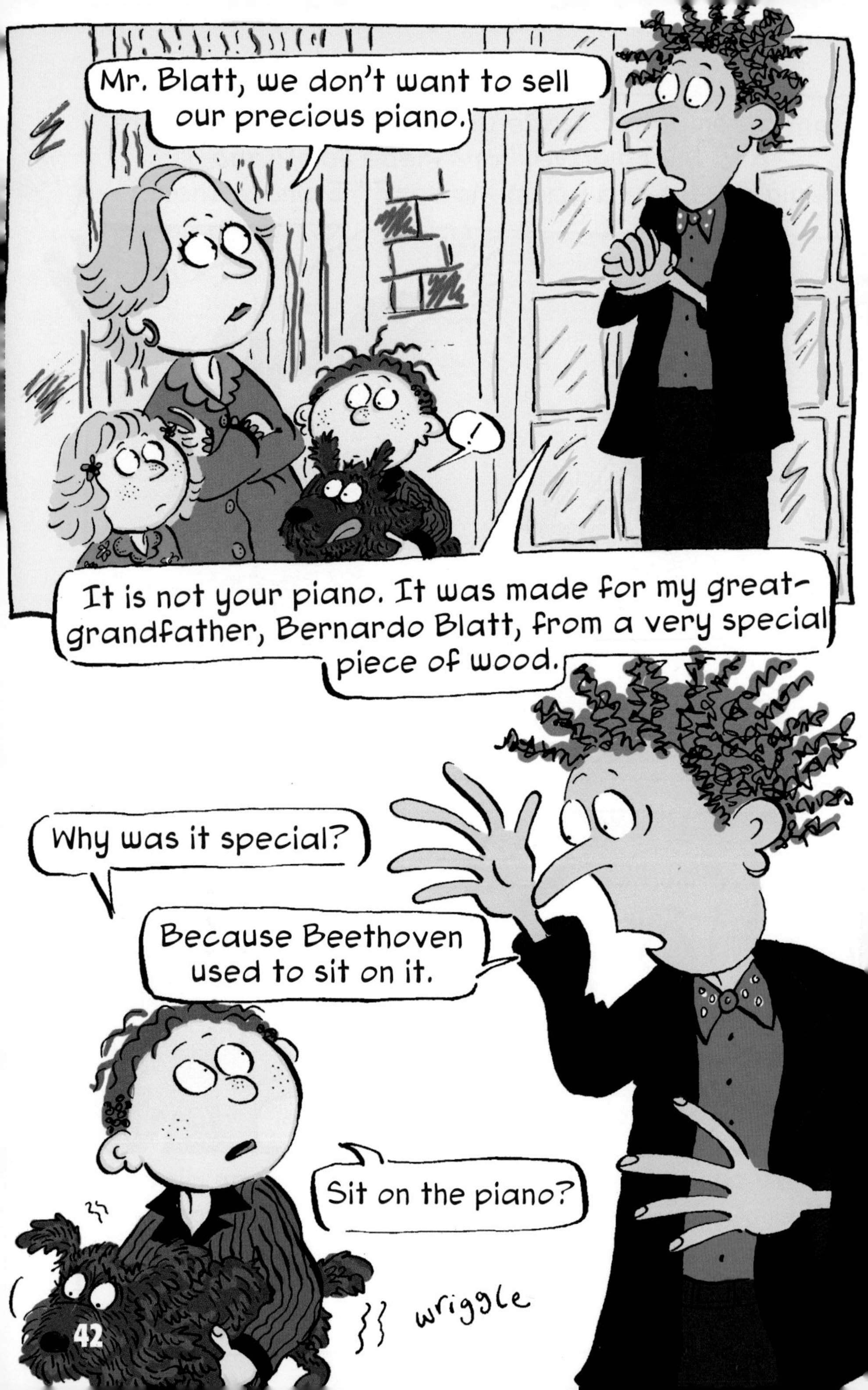
Mr. Blatt, we don't want to sell our precious piano.
!
It is not your piano. It was made for my great-grandfather, Bernardo Blatt, from a very special piece of wood.
Why was it special?
Because Beethoven used to sit on it.
Sit on the piano?
wriggle

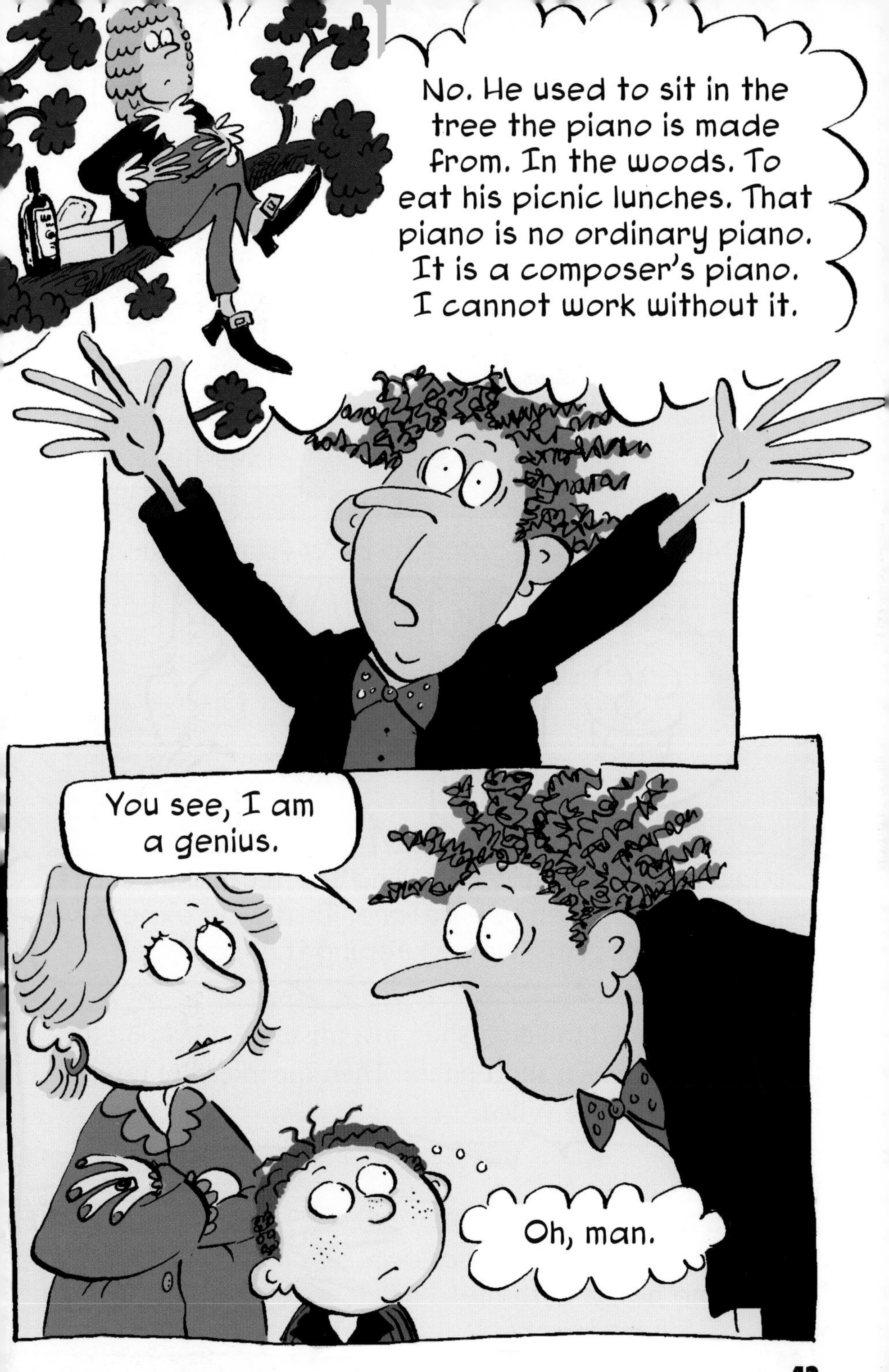
No. He used to sit in the tree the piano is made from. In the woods. To eat his picnic lunches. That piano is no ordinary piano. It is a composer's piano. I cannot work without it.
You see, I am a genius.
Oh, man.

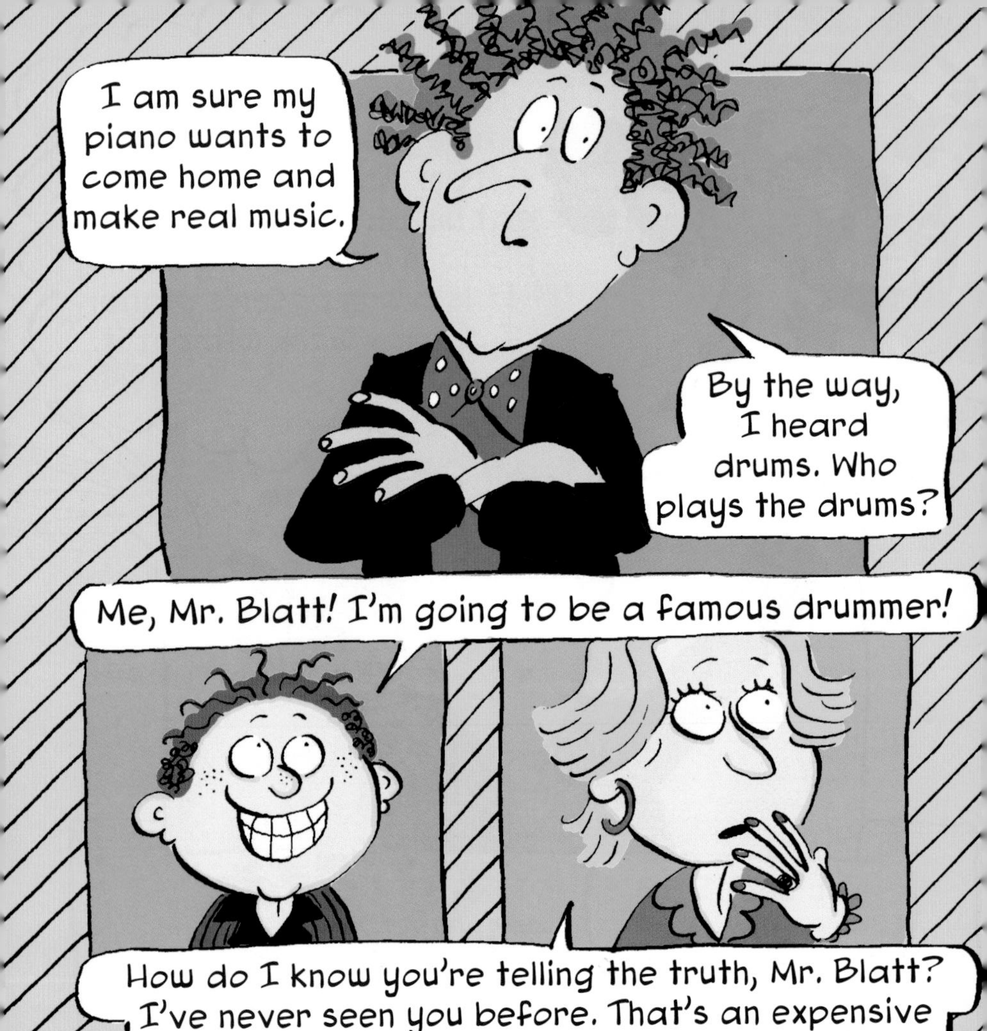
I am sure my piano wants to come home and make real music.
By the way, I heard drums. Who plays the drums?
Me, Mr. Blatt! I'm going to be a famous drummer!
How do I know you're telling the truth, Mr. Blatt? I've never seen you before. That's an expensive piano, and we're keeping it. Goodbye!

Mom slammed the door shut, just missing Ludwig Blatt's nose. There was a short pause. Then the mail slot flipped open and a voice yelled.

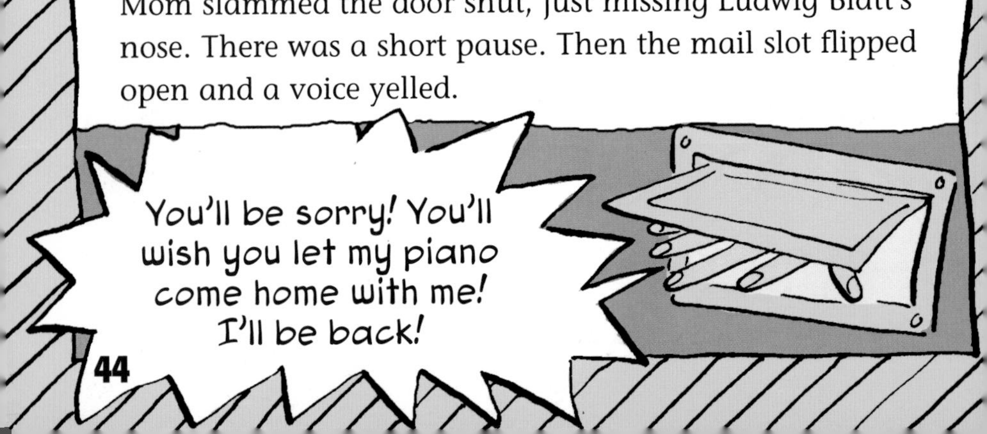
You'll be sorry! You'll wish you let my piano come home with me! I'll be back!

Chapter Seven

That night Lenny didn't sleep at all. The piano wailed and roared and howled. Lenny hid under his covers with Bonzo, but still couldn't sleep.

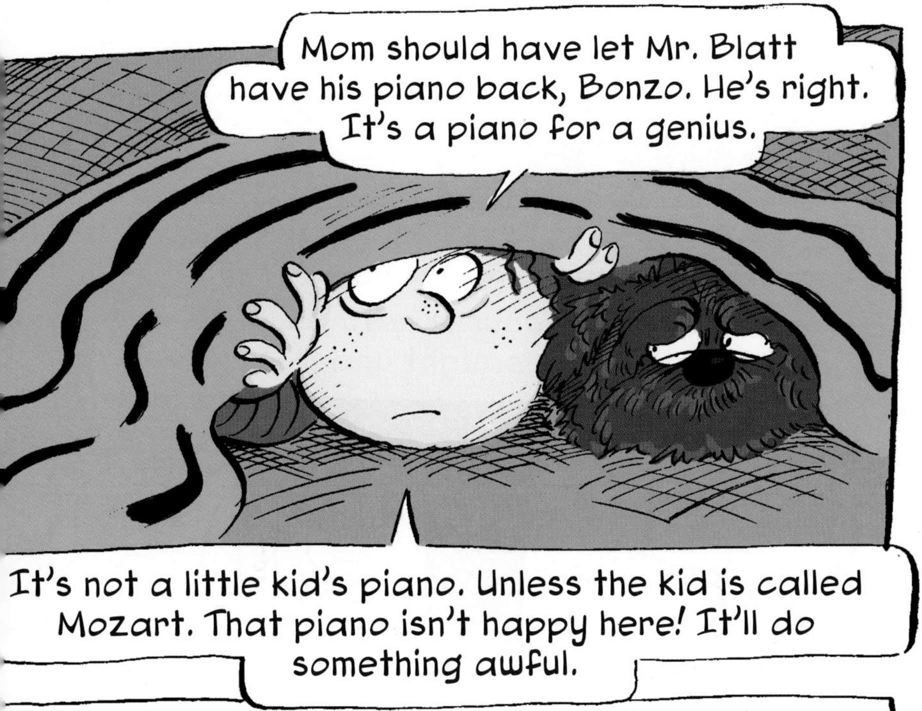
Mom should have let Mr. Blatt have his piano back, Bonzo. He's right. It's a piano for a genius.
It's not a little kid's piano. Unless the kid is called Mozart. That piano isn't happy here! It'll do something awful.

Lenny fell asleep when morning came. He slept late. It was noon when he ate breakfast.

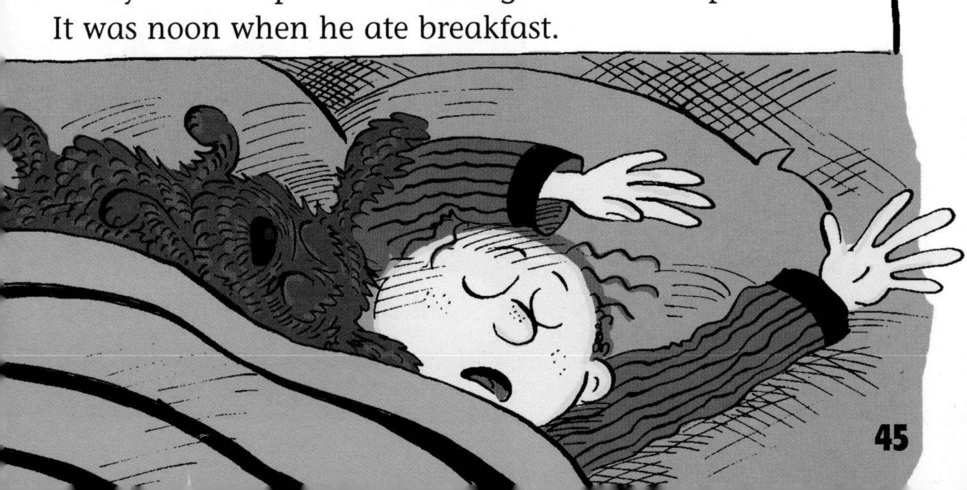

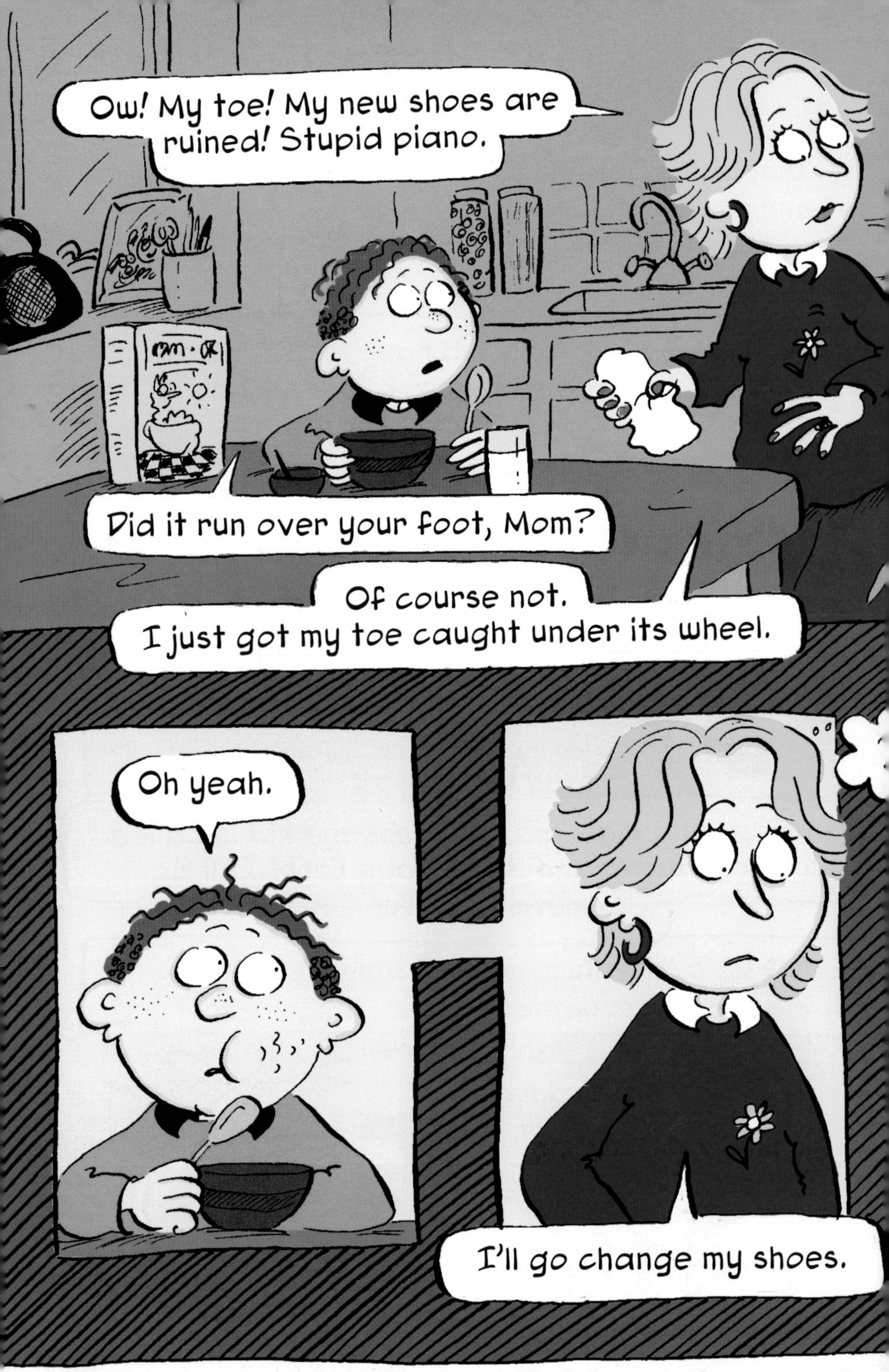
Ow! My toe! My new shoes are ruined! Stupid piano.
Did it run over your foot, Mom?
Of course not. I just got my toe caught under its wheel.
Oh yeah.
I'll go change my shoes.

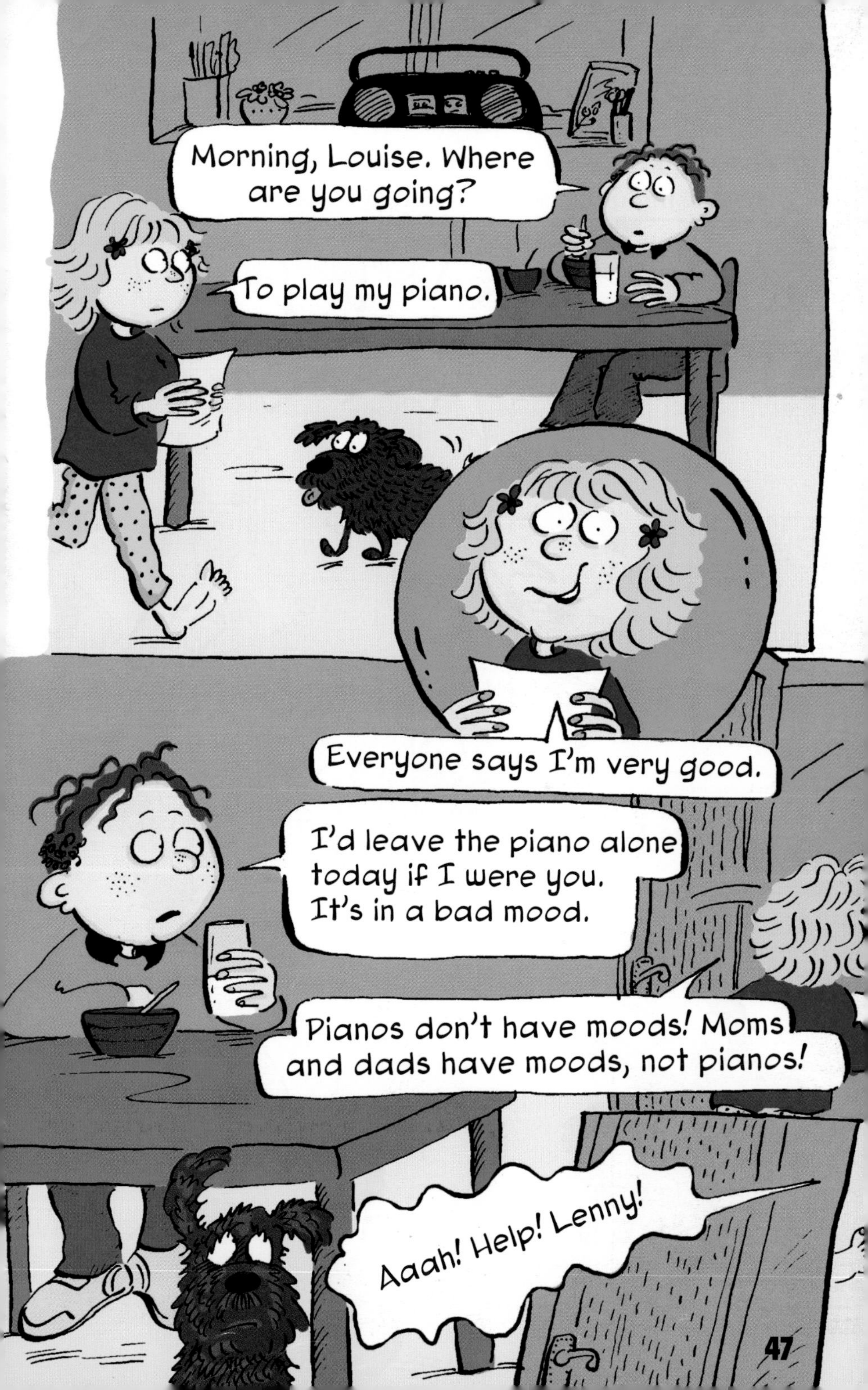

Morning, Louise. Where are you going?
To play my piano.
Everyone says I'm very good.
I'd leave the piano alone today if I were you. It's in a bad mood.
Pianos don't have moods! Moms and dads have moods, not pianos!
Aaah! Help! Lenny!

Lenny dashed into the room. He saw a great big pair of jaws, wide open, like a shark. The piano was trying to eat Louise! Its keys were snapping and chomping. Louise's legs were sticking out from between its keys.

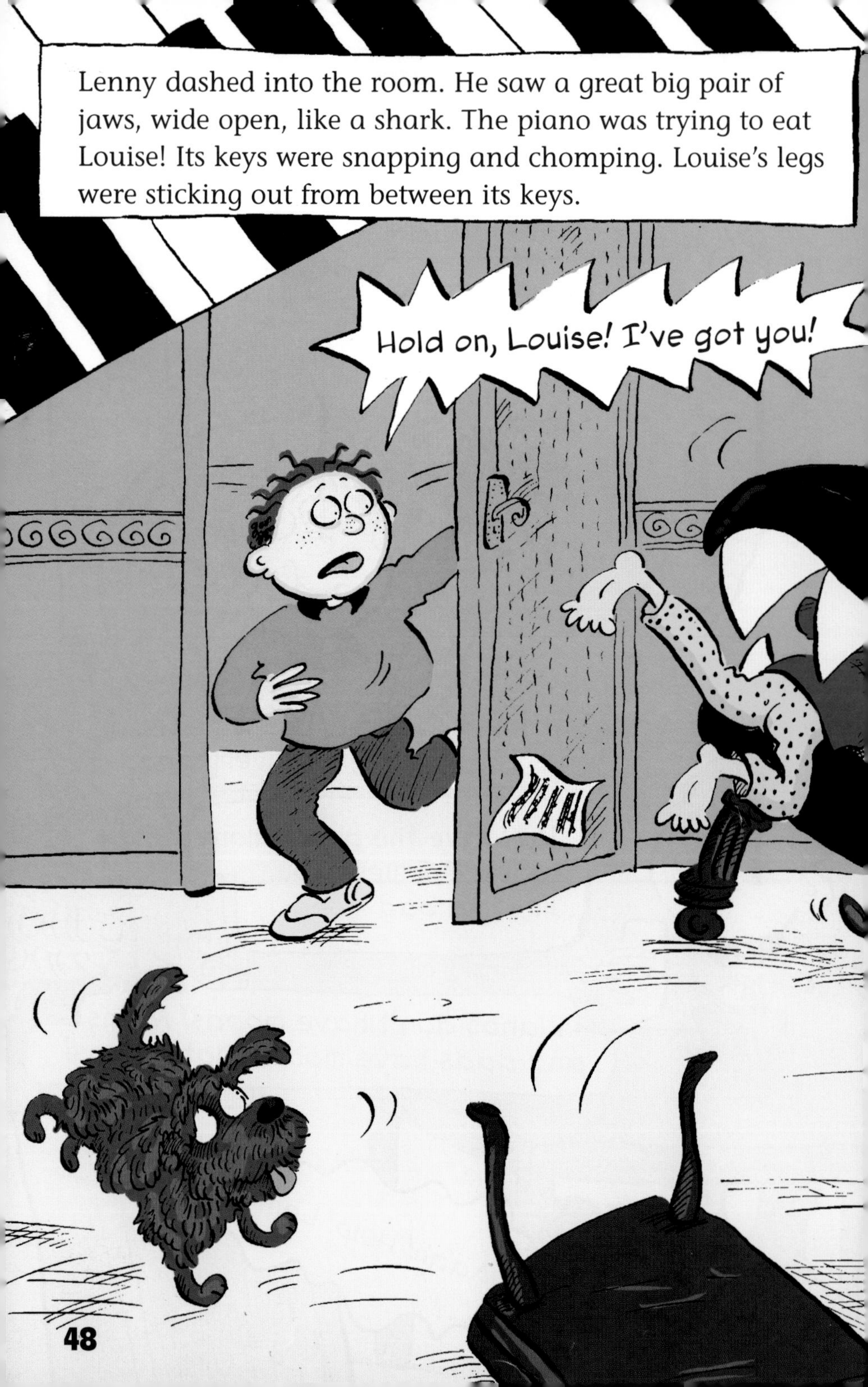
Hold on, Louise! I've got you!

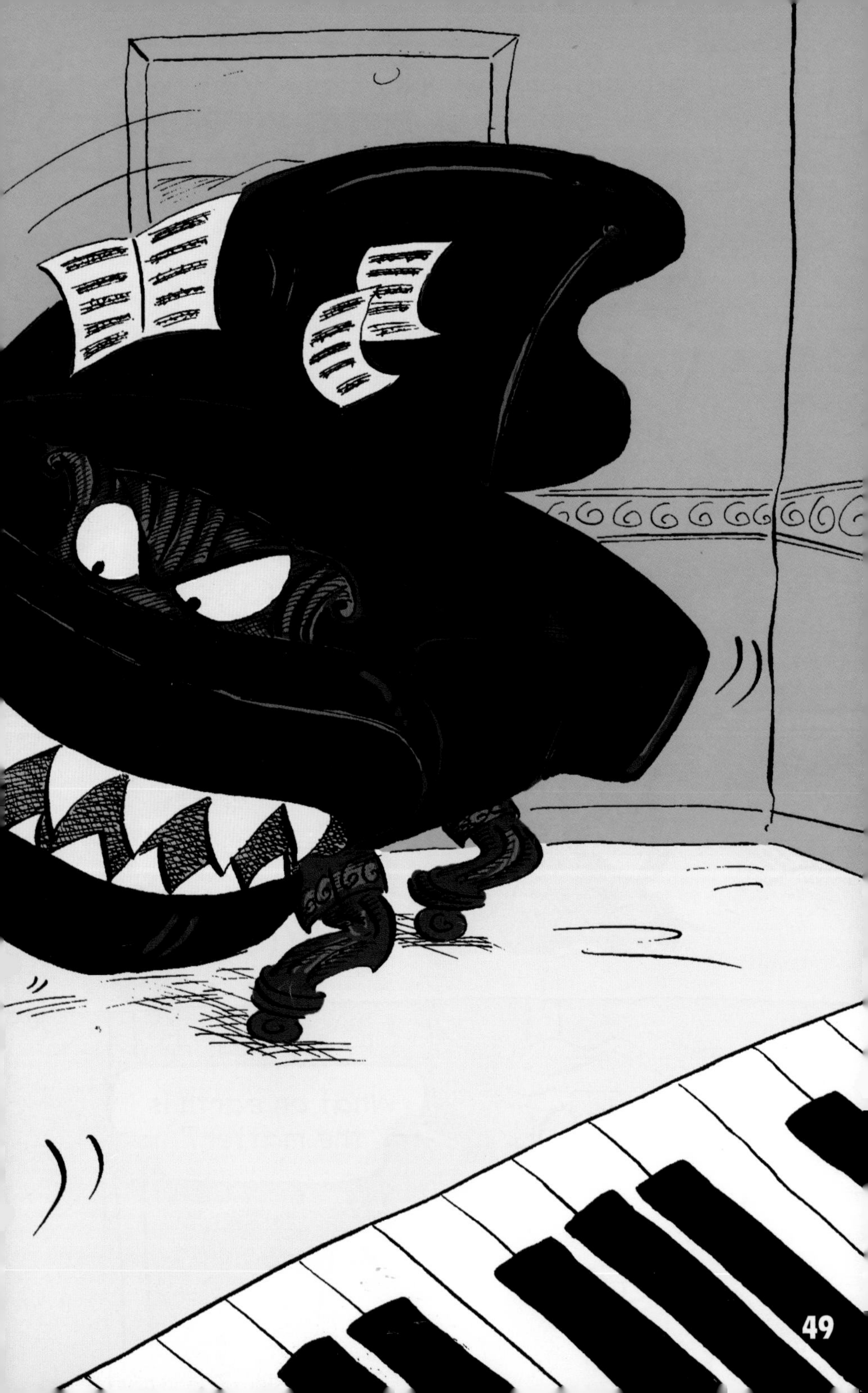

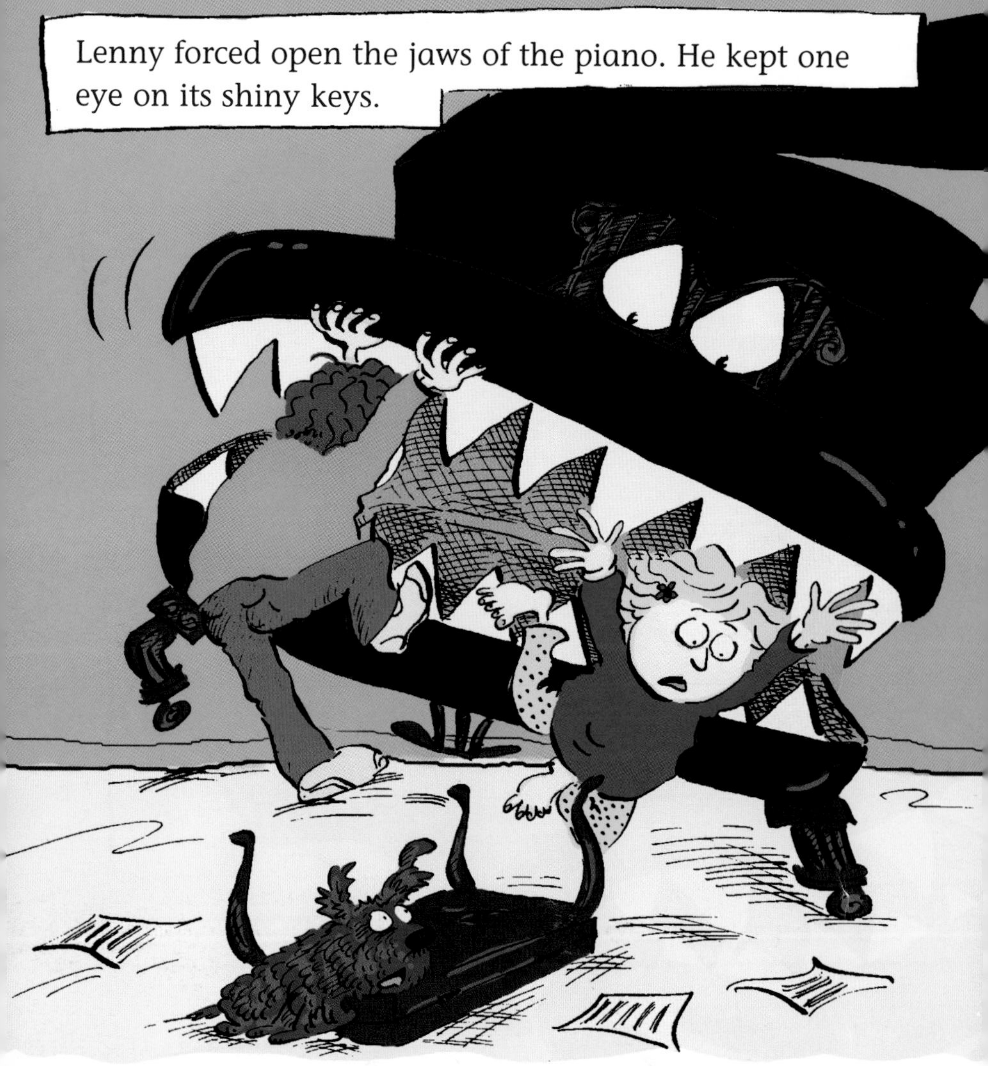
Lenny forced open the jaws of the piano. He kept one eye on its shiny keys.

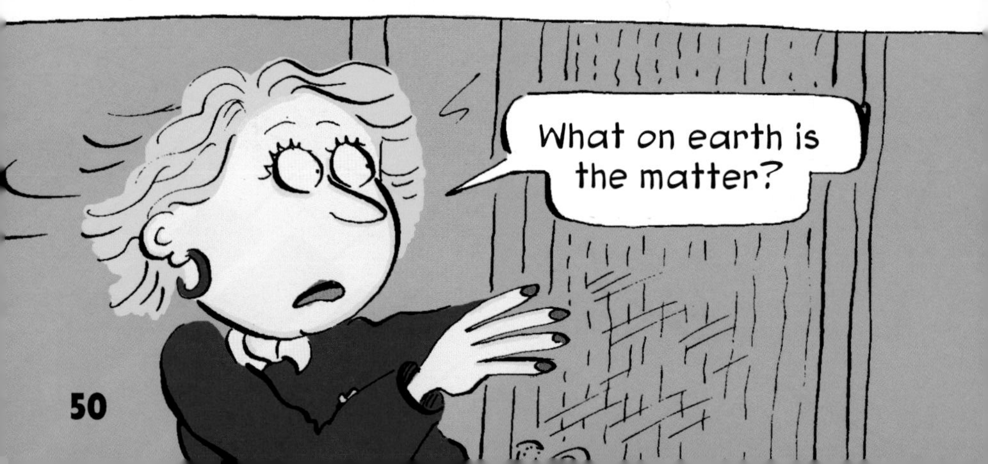
What on earth is the matter?

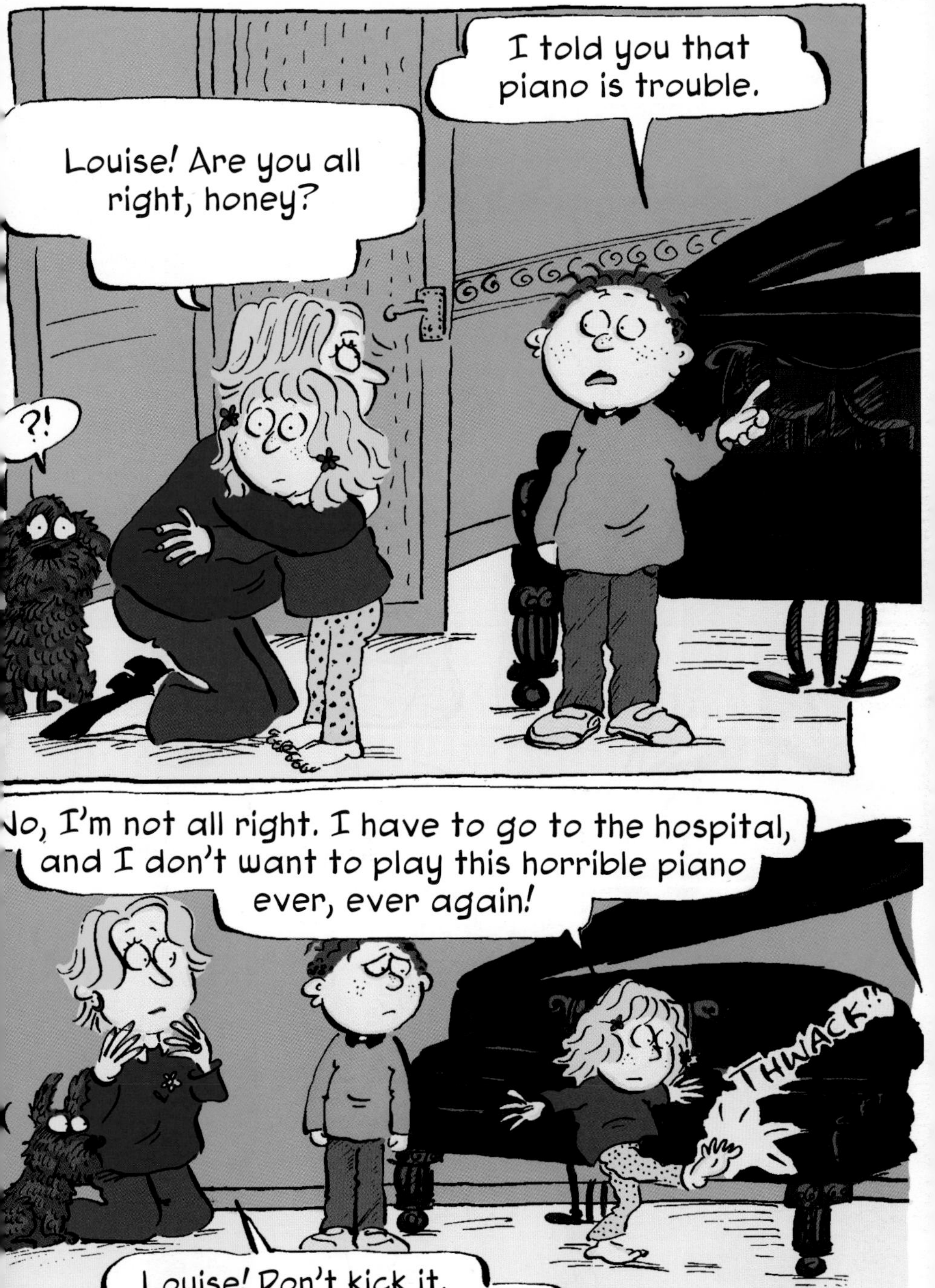

Louise! Are you all right, honey?
I told you that piano is trouble.
?!
No, I'm not all right. I have to go to the hospital, and I don't want to play this horrible piano ever, ever again!
THWACK!!
Louise! Don't kick it. It's probably an antique.

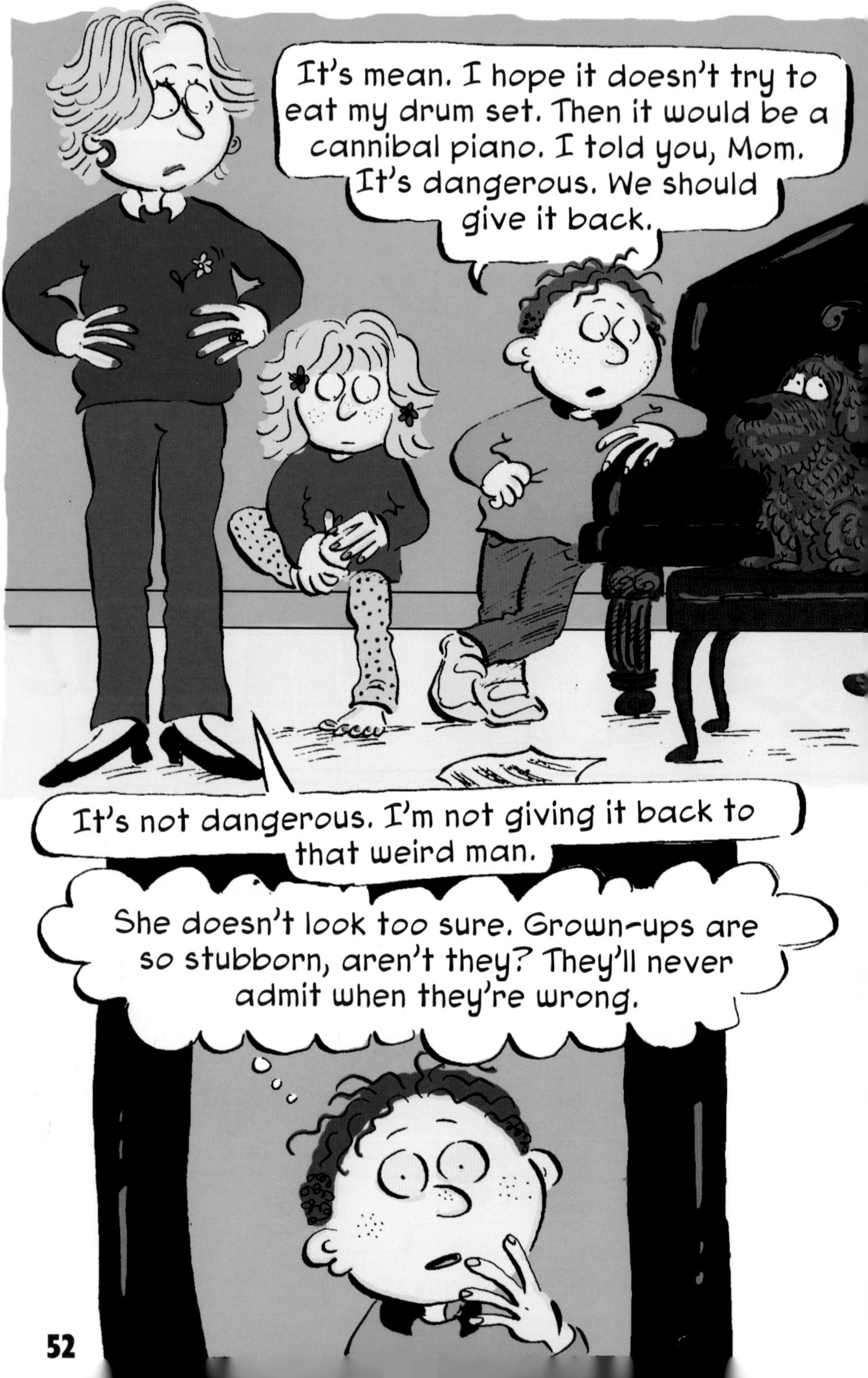
It's mean. I hope it doesn't try to eat my drum set. Then it would be a cannibal piano. I told you, Mom. It's dangerous. We should give it back.
It's not dangerous. I'm not giving it back to that weird man.
She doesn't look too sure. Grown-ups are so stubborn, aren't they? They'll never admit when they're wrong.

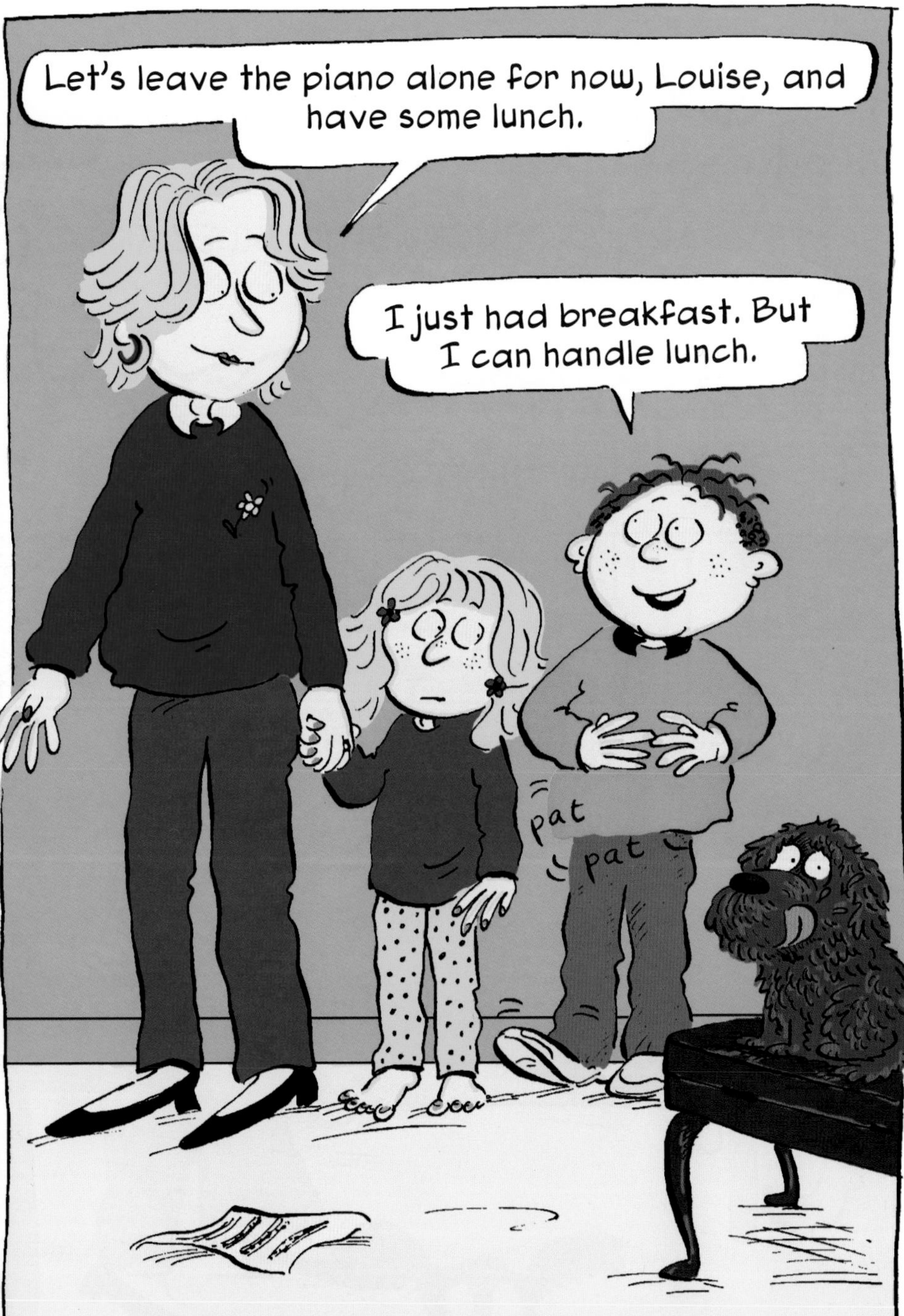
Let's leave the piano alone for now, Louise, and have some lunch.
I just had breakfast. But I can handle lunch.
pat
pat

Just as they sat down with their plates of food, they heard a crazy noise.

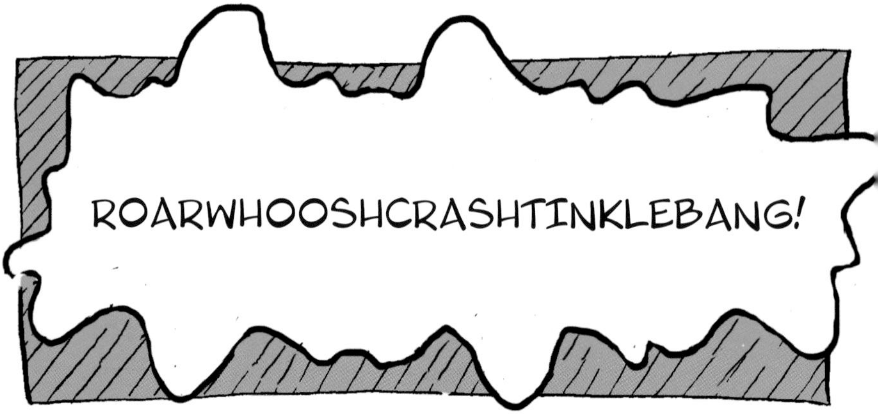
ROARWHOOSHCRASHTINKLEBANG!

Then they heard silence. An awful silence.

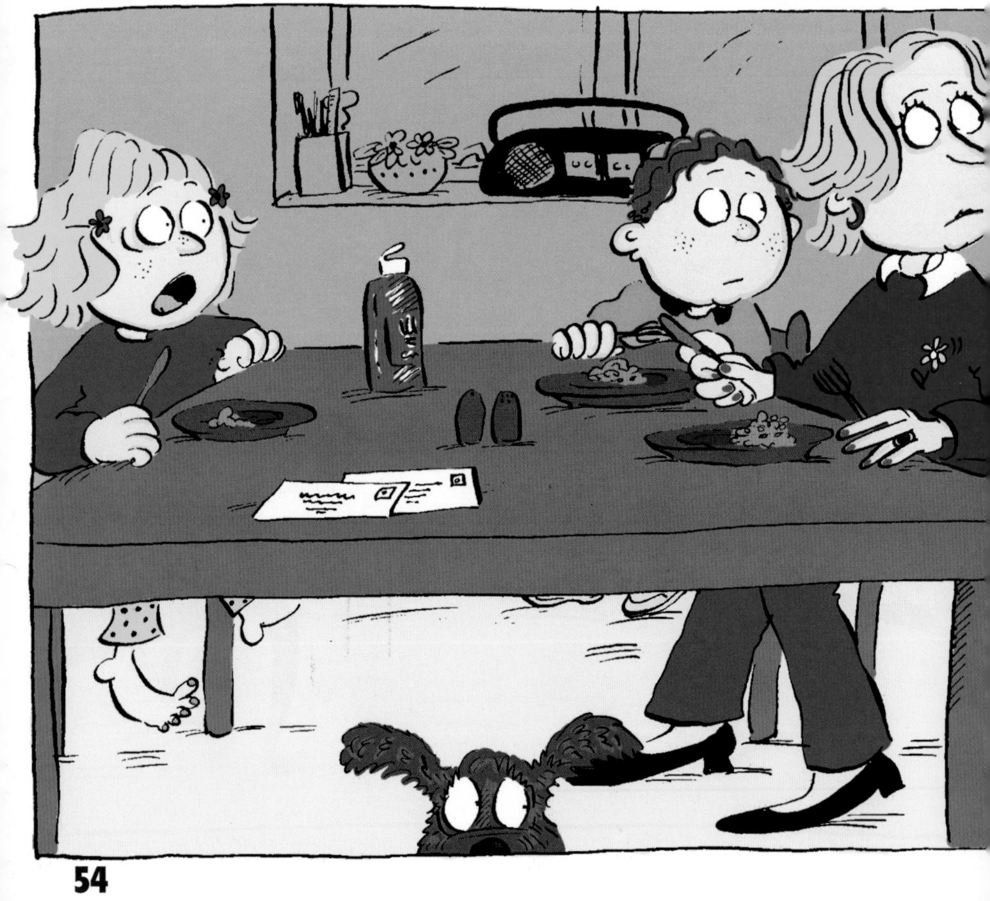

Chapter Eight

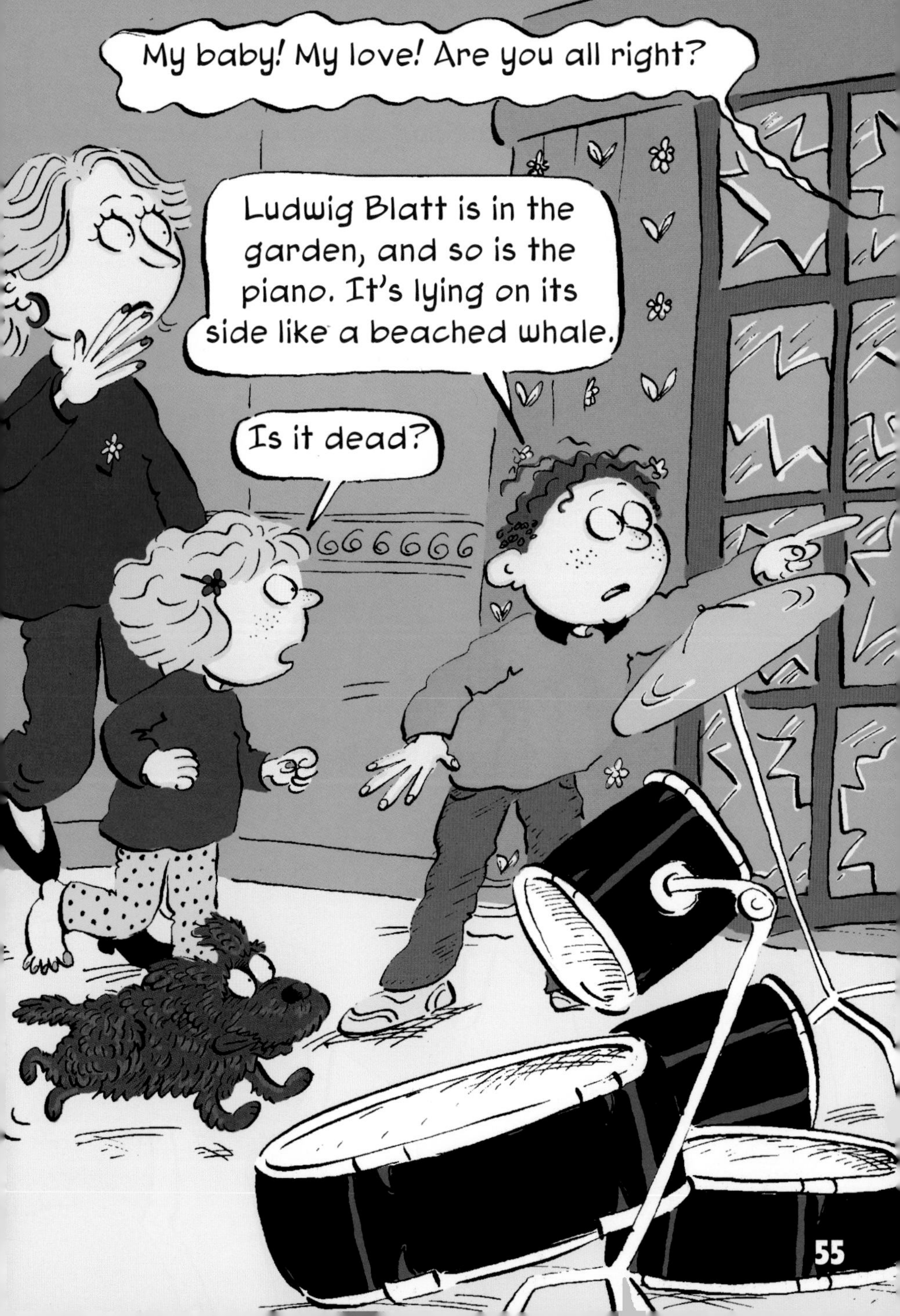
My baby! My love! Are you all right?
Ludwig Blatt is in the garden, and so is the piano. It's lying on its side like a beached whale.
Is it dead?

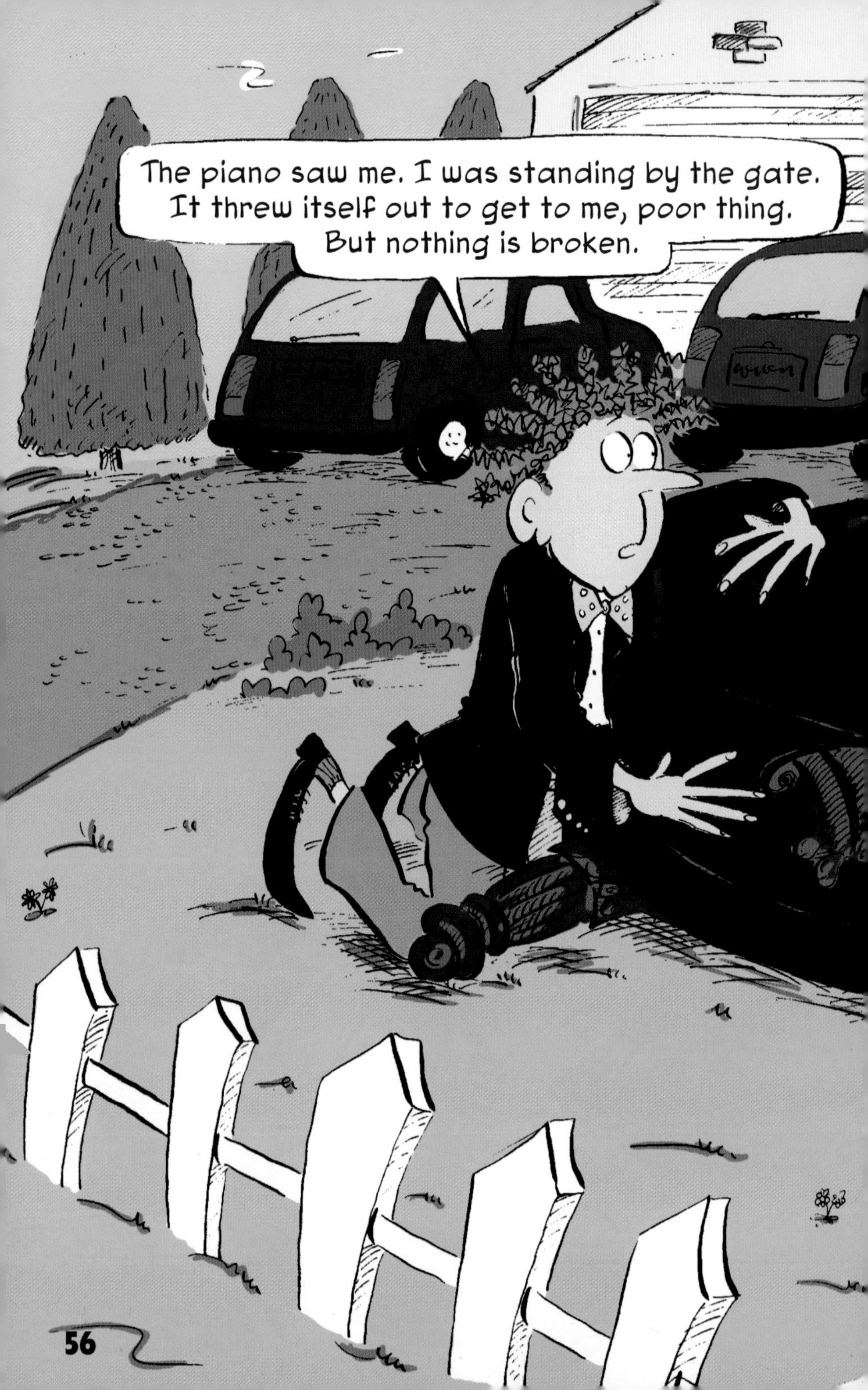
The piano saw me. I was standing by the gate. It threw itself out to get to me, poor thing. But nothing is broken.

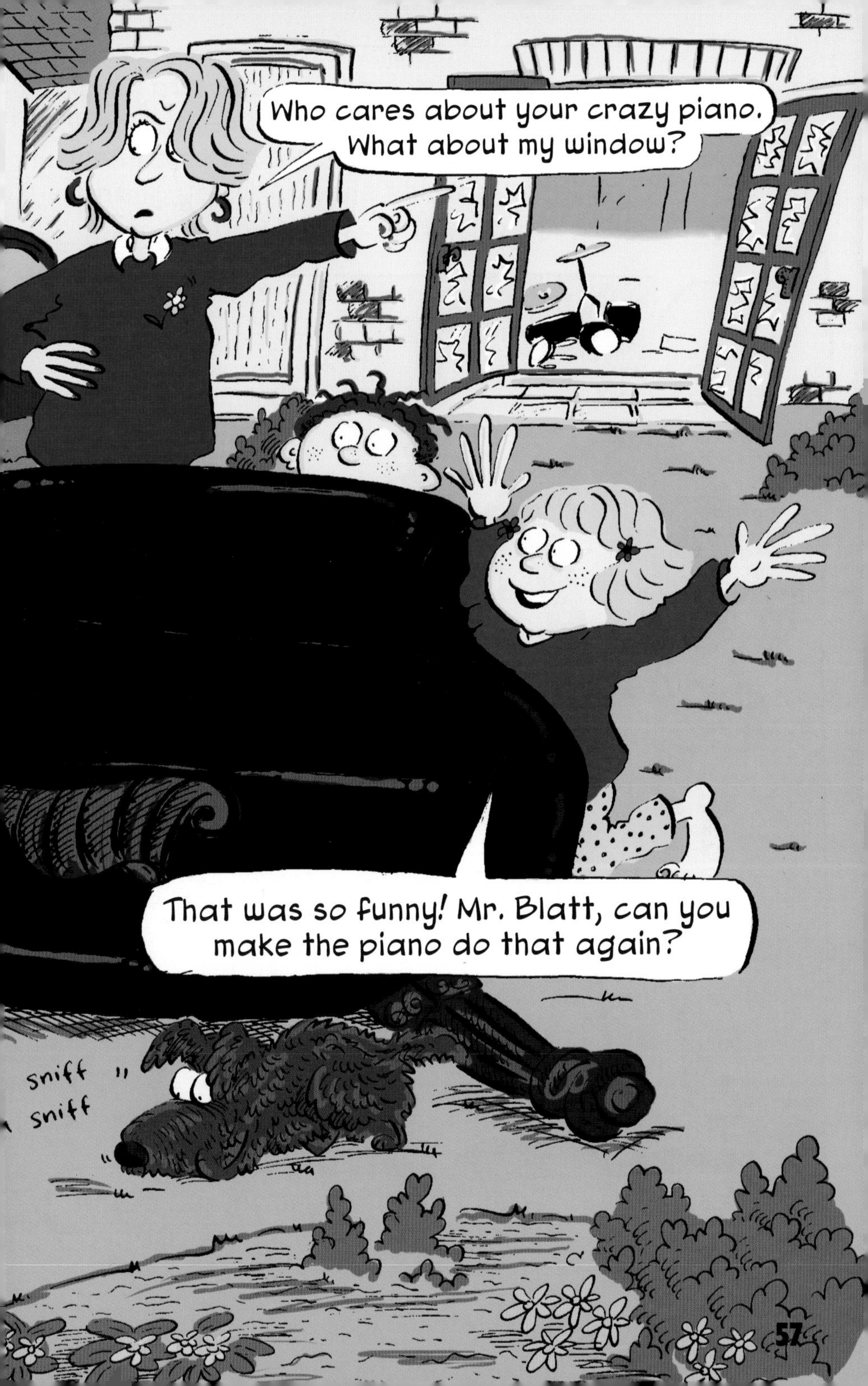
Who cares about your crazy piano. What about my window?
That was so funny! Mr. Blatt, can you make the piano do that again?
sniff
sniff

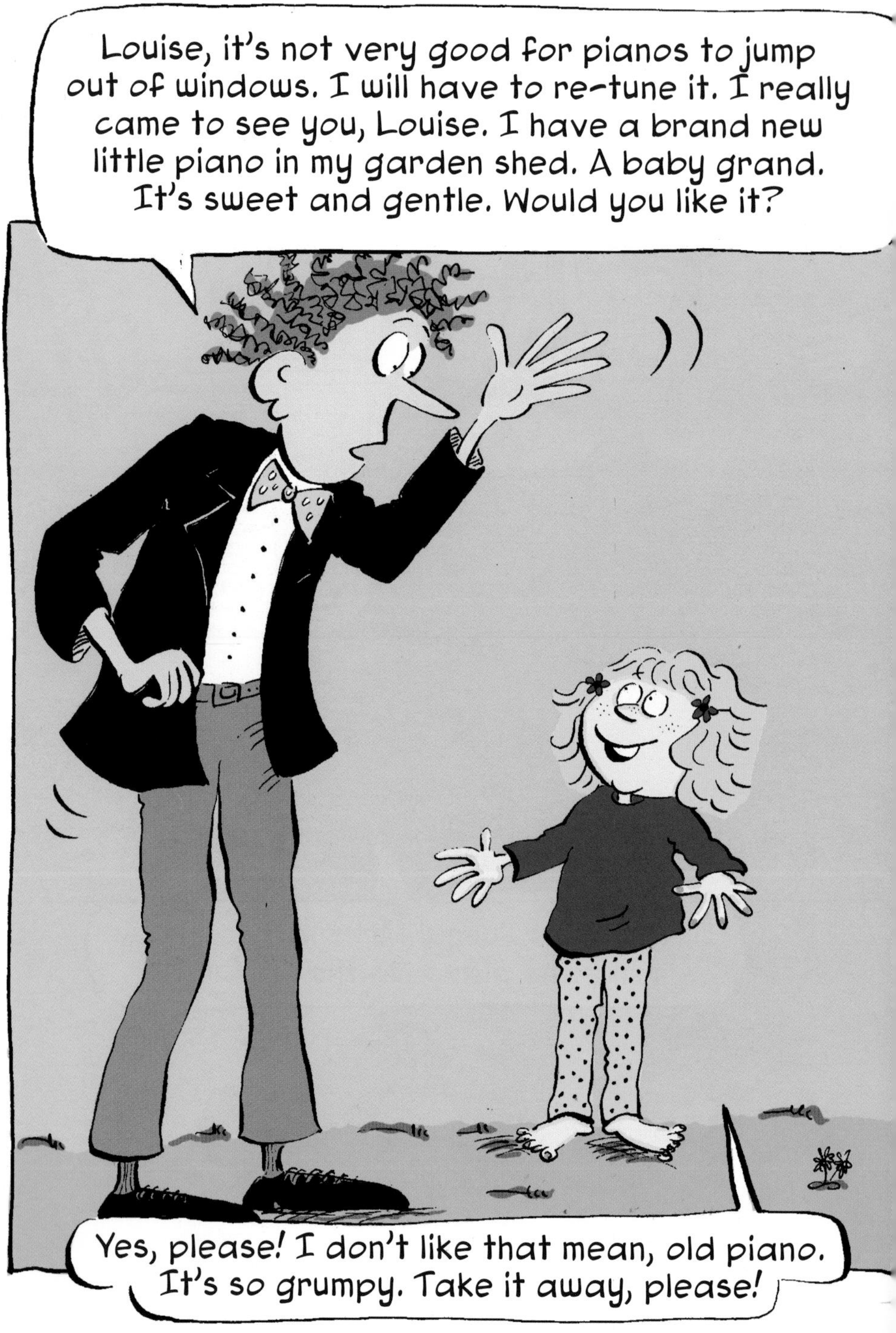
Louise, it's not very good for pianos to jump out of windows. I will have to re-tune it. I really came to see you, Louise. I have a brand new little piano in my garden shed. A baby grand. It's sweet and gentle. Would you like it?
Yes, please! I don't like that mean, old piano. It's so grumpy. Take it away, please!

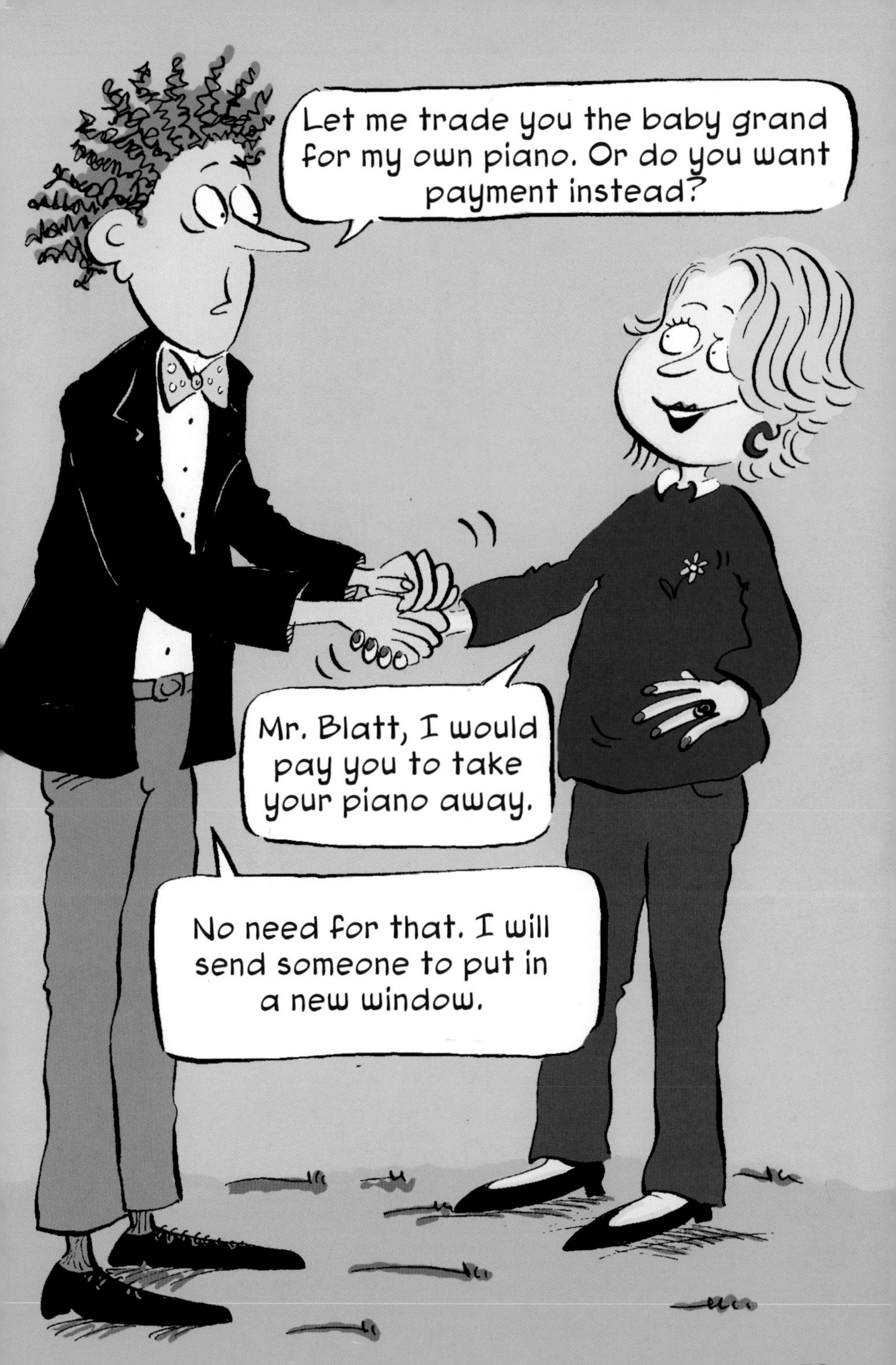
Let me trade you the baby grand for my own piano. Or do you want payment instead?
Mr. Blatt, I would pay you to take your piano away.
No need for that. I will send someone to put in a new window.

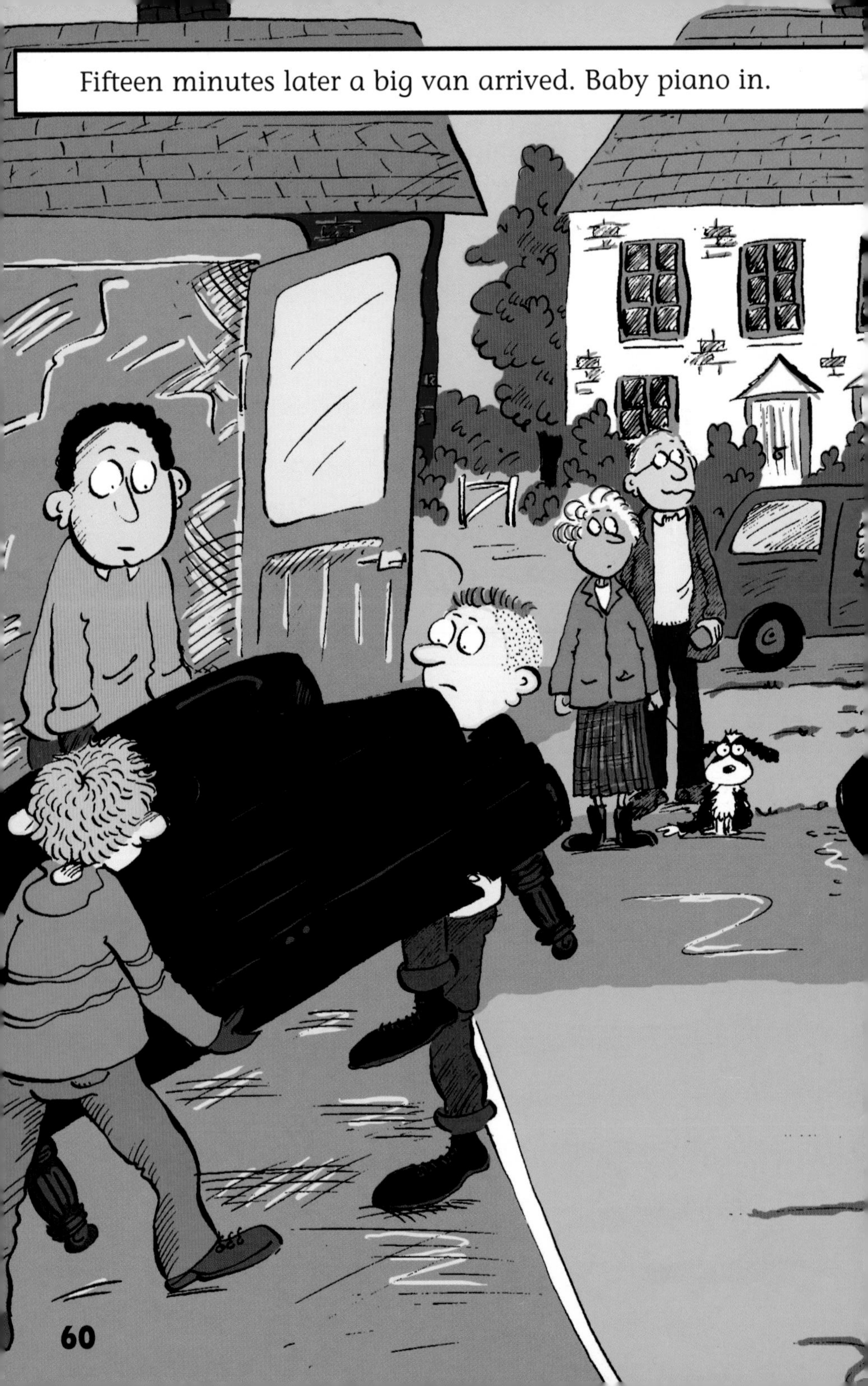
Fifteen minutes later a big van arrived. Baby piano in.

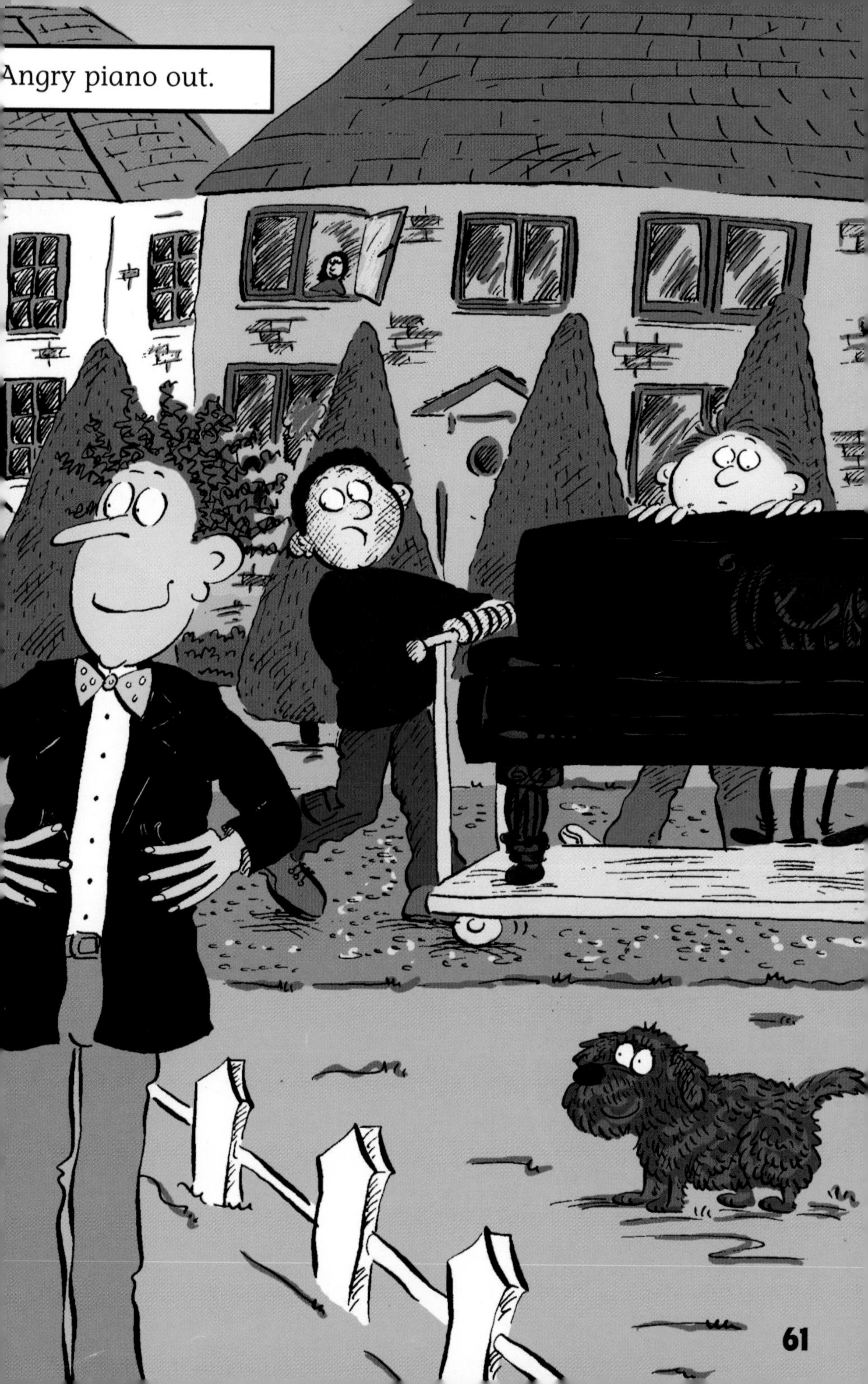
Angry piano out.

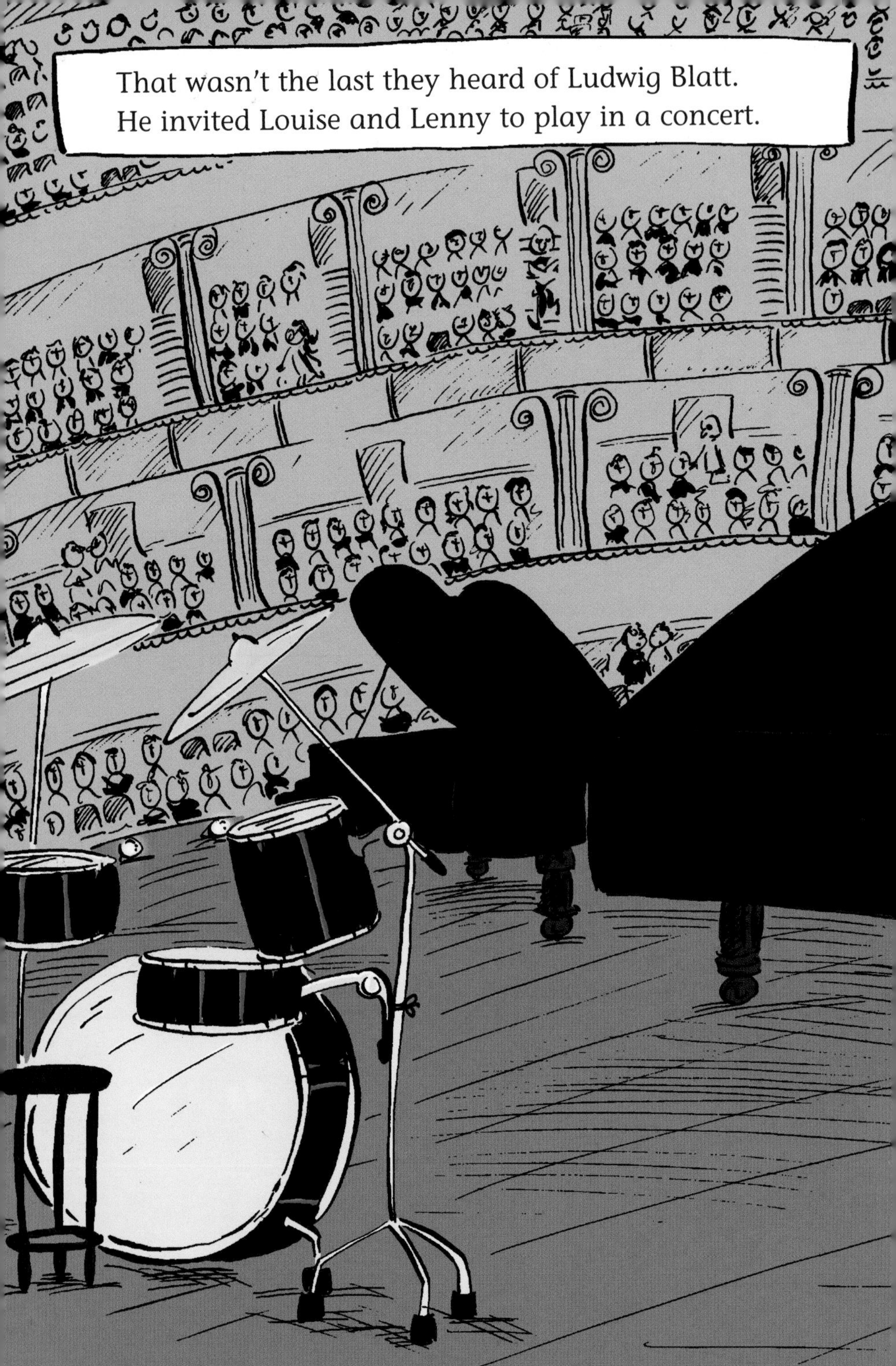
That wasn't the last they heard of Ludwig Blatt.
He invited Louise and Lenny to play in a concert.

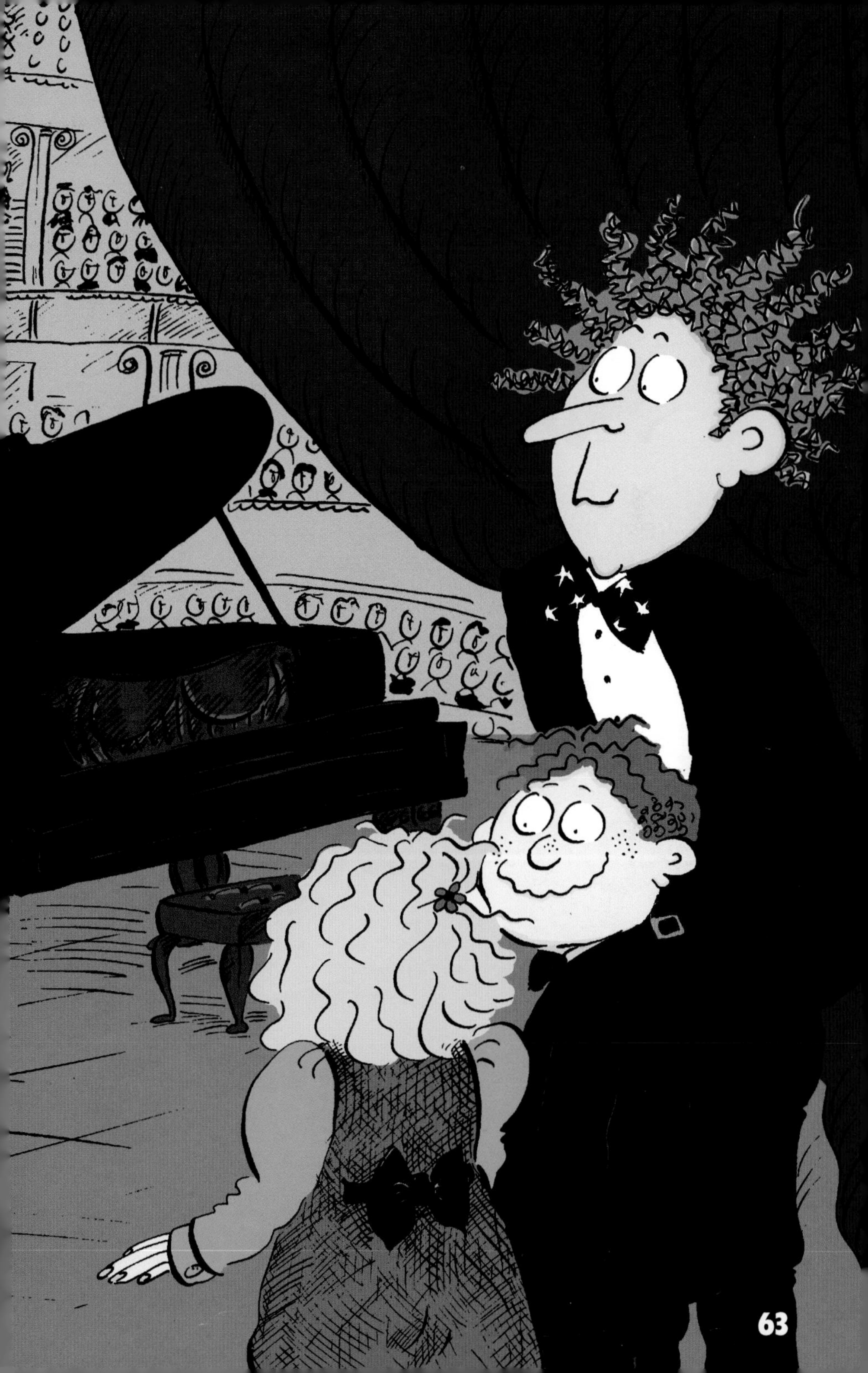

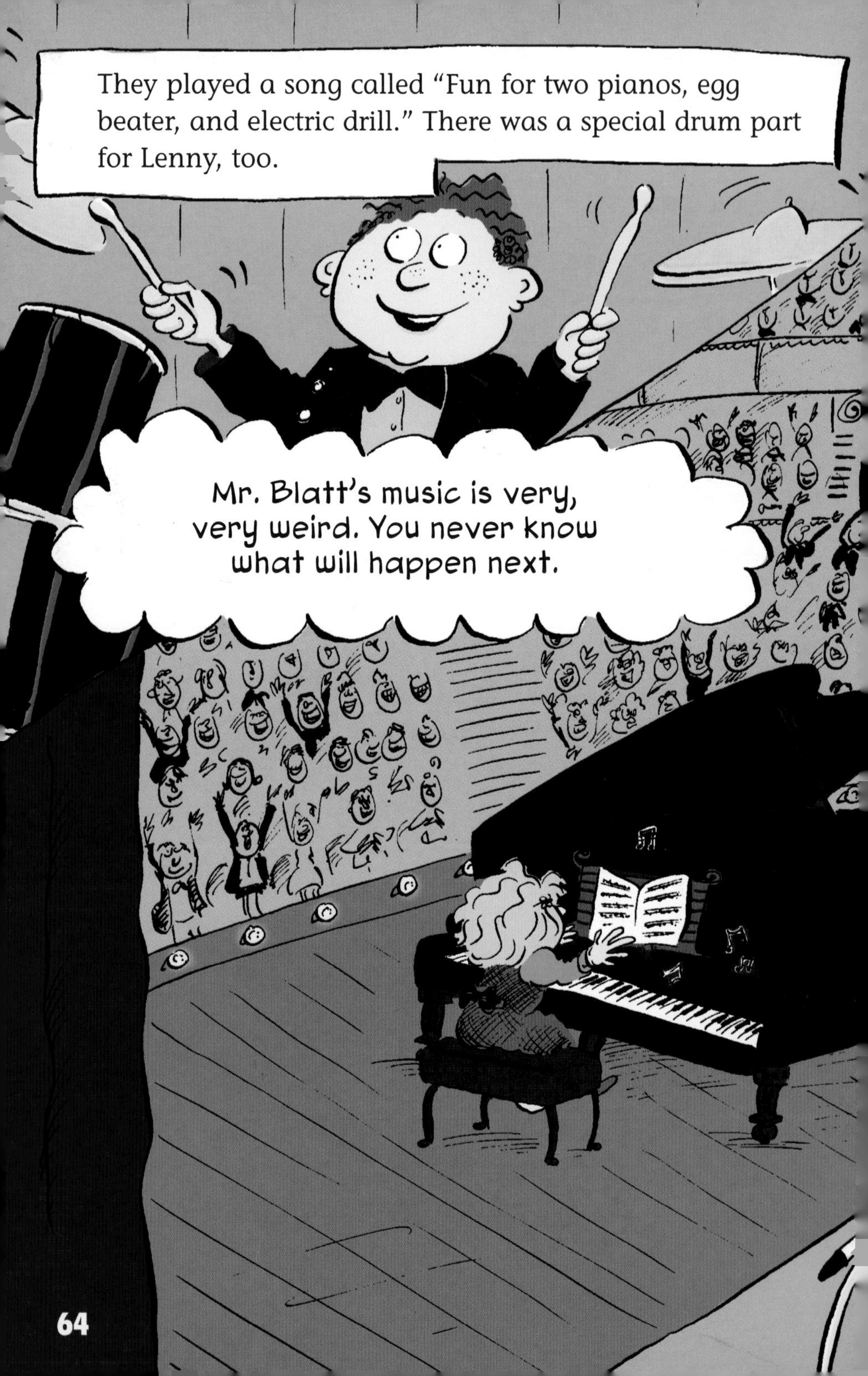
They played a song called "Fun for two pianos, egg beater, and electric drill." There was a special drum part for Lenny, too.
Mr. Blatt's music is very, very weird. You never know what will happen next.

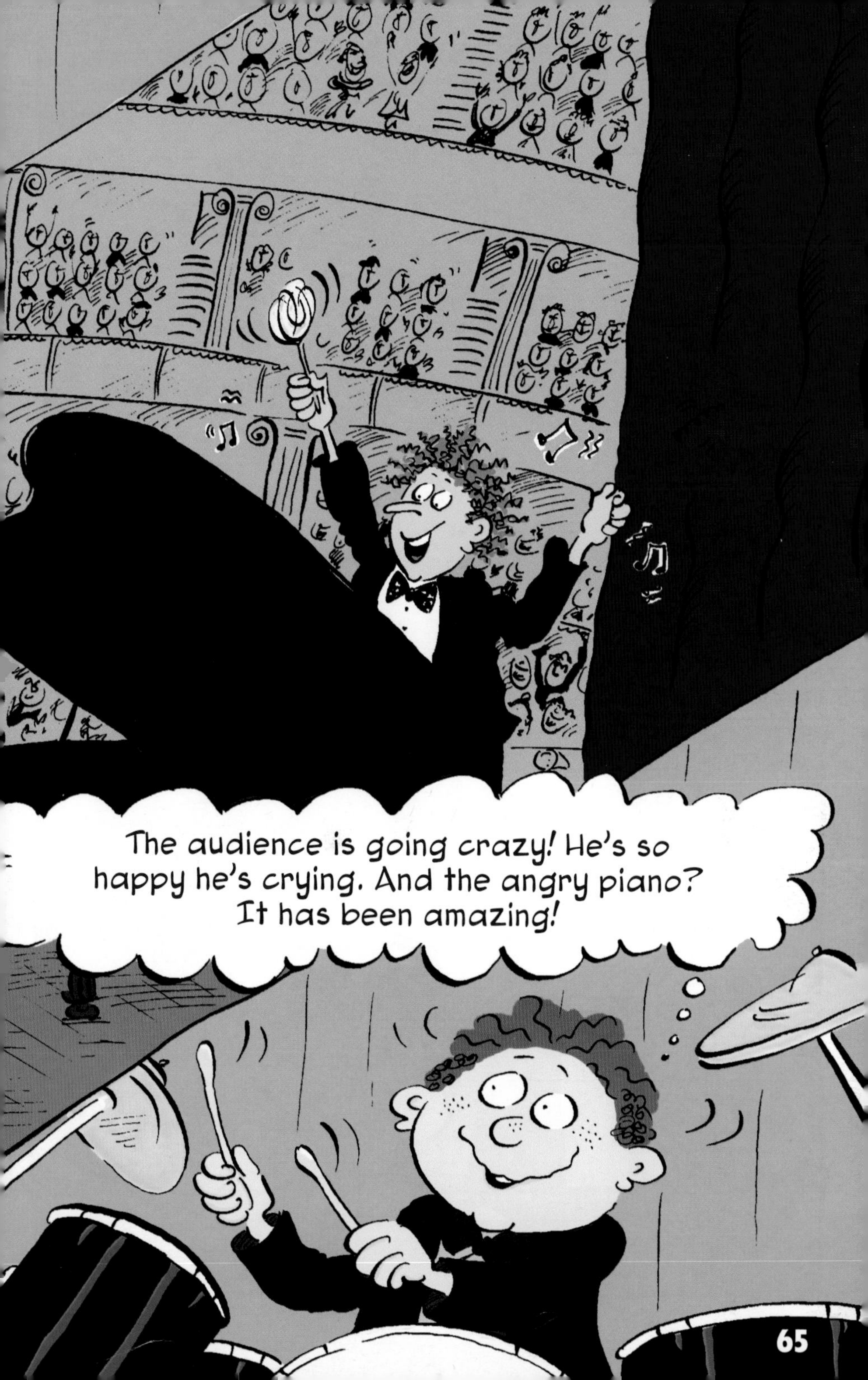
The audience is going crazy! He's so happy he's crying. And the angry piano? It has been amazing!

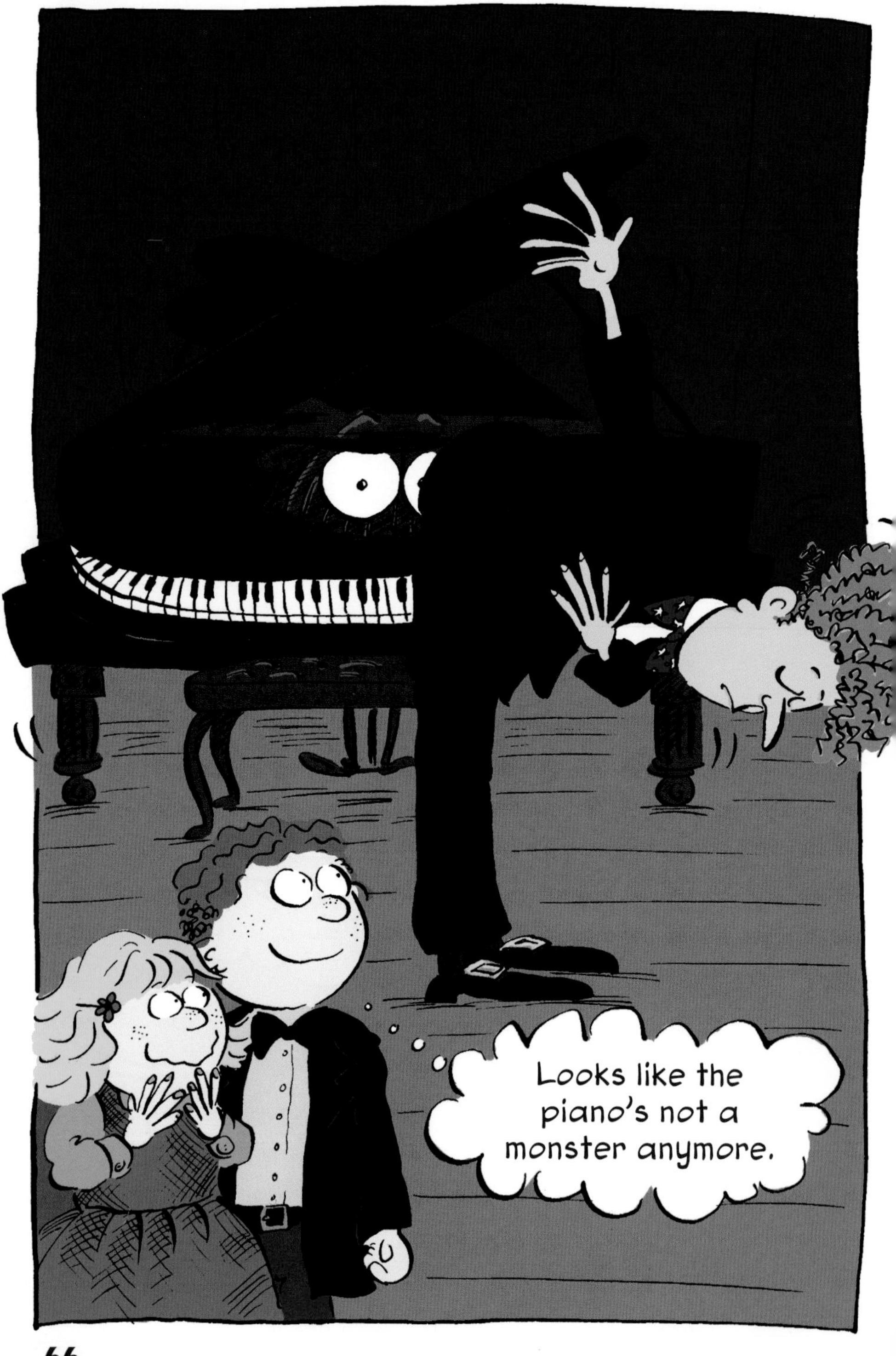
Looks like the piano's not a monster anymore.

ABOUT THE AUTHOR

Caroline Pitcher grew up in East Yorkshire, England. She loved playing outside and reading nature books. This love of the outdoors is portrayed in many of her books. Caroline writes books for children and young adults. She enjoys going to schools and talking to kids. She now lives in Derbyshire, England.

ABOUT THE ILLUSTRATOR

Bridget MacKeith says that being an illustrator is the only thing she has ever wanted to be. Although she once thought of being an opera singer! MacKeith's artwork appears in dozens of children's books. She currently lives in a small town in the middle of the Salisbury Plain in England, with her husband, Gareth, her two children, and a big, hairy Newfoundland dog named Rudi. She also illustrates "a lot of cards for Hallmark."

GLOSSARY

antique (an-TEEK)—an object that is valuable because it is very old and rare

cannibal (KAN-uh-buhl)—someone who eats human flesh (or the flesh of its own species, if it is not a human)

composer (kuhm-POE-zur)—someone who writes or creates musical works

duet (doo-ET)—a piece of music that is performed by two instruments, or sung by two people

genius (JEEN-yuhss)—someone who has great natural ability to think and create

piccolo (PIK-uh-low)—a musical instrument that is shaped like a small flute, and makes a high, piercing sound

tune (TOON)—a song, or simple piece of music

villain (VIL-uhn)—an evil or wicked person

INTERNET SITES

Do you want to know more about subjects related to this book? Or are you interested in learning about other topics? Then check out FactHound, a fun, easy way to find Internet sites.

Our investigative staff has already sniffed out great sites for you!

Here's how to use FactHound:

1. Visit *www.facthound.com*

2. Select your grade level.

3. To learn more about subjects related to this book, type in the book's ISBN number: **1598890875**.

4. Click the **Fetch It** button.

FactHound will fetch the best Internet sites for you.

DISCUSSION QUESTIONS

1. What would you do if you found out
   that your family had a "monster piano?"
   Explain your reasoning.

2. Discuss what creates the piano's moods.
   Give examples from the text and/or pictures.

3. What do you think of the parents in this
   story? Are their actions and responses
   believable? Why or why not? Explain.

4. Does Mr. Blatt's situation make sense?
   Why or why not?

WRITING PROMPTS

1. Imagine that Lenny's family keeps the monster piano. Write about what happens.

2. Write a story in which an object in your house comes to life. Describe the object and what it does.

3. Review the names of Ludwig Blatt's compositions on pages 41 and 64. Combine musical terms, different names, and odd sounds to create the titles of three more songs that Lenny and Louise could play.

ALSO BY
C. PITCHER

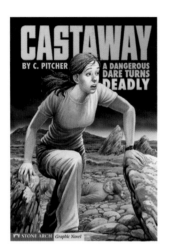

Castaway

Six kids on a geography trip are cut off by the sea. One of them is hurt, it's the middle of the night, and they have only themselves to blame.

STONE ARCH BOOKS,
151 Good Counsel Hill Drive, Mankato, MN 56001
1-800-421-7731
www.stonearchbooks.com